HIS DARKEST CRAVING

THE CURSED ONES 1

TIFFANY ROBERTS

Tiffany Roberts

authortiffanyroberts@gmail.com

Cover Illustration by Linda Noeran

Art by Mar

❀ Created with Vellum

To the one I crave.

CHAPTER ONE

SOPHIE PULLED up the collar of her coat as she watched the movers step off the porch of her new home.

Home.

That wasn't quite the right word to describe this place. This was a hideaway, somewhere she could isolate herself and find some way to heal the many wounds she'd endured over the last five years. It was a quaint, rustic little cabin in the woods, a far cry from the city and suburbs she'd lived in for most of her life, but she'd do all she could to make it hers.

One of the movers walked toward their truck while the other approached Sophie, a clipboard in his left hand. She fought the urge to step back, lower her eyes, and make herself as small as possible. Drawing in a deep breath, she grounded herself.

They're not all bad. They're not all like him.

She released the breath, forced herself to meet the man's eyes, and returned his smile.

"That should do it!" he said, holding the clipboard out to her. "Just need a signature, and we'll be on our way."

Sophie accepted the clipboard and glanced over the work

order before signing her name at the bottom. The services had been prepaid, and everything looked to be accurate. She handed it back to the mover. "Thank you, especially for coming all the way out here. I know the roads are difficult. I can't imagine getting that truck back here in one piece."

"We've been through worse, and the boss pays us by the hour. That means we can take the time to be extra careful." His grin was warm and friendly. "We didn't break any of your stuff, and that's all that really matters."

"That's always a good thing." She slipped her hand into her coat pocket, pulled out a couple folded bills, and held them out to him. "Thanks again, really."

He tucked the clipboard under his arm and accepted the tip. "Wow, thanks. Hope you enjoy your new place." He stepped back and glanced around them. "Definitely beautiful out here. Have a great day, Miss Davis."

Striding across the driveway, he climbed into the passenger side of the truck's cab to join his companion. The engine rumbled to life as he tugged his door shut. It was a jarring sound in the otherwise serene woods, but the truck was quickly on its way, jouncing along the dirt road toward the old highway half a mile away. Sophie remained where she stood until she could no longer see the truck between the trees.

She skimmed her gaze over the surrounding trees. Their vibrant red, orange, and yellow foliage rustled in the breeze, which sent more leaves on a lazy, tumbling journey to the ground.

"This is it," she said with a sigh. Sophie was truly alone now, in the middle of nowhere. Most people would've thought her insane to have gone to such an extreme, but she *needed* the peace and quiet, needed a sanctuary in which she could heal and reclaim her life without living under a constant shadow of fear.

She turned back to the house. It was a small, single-story log cabin with a screen door and a roofed porch, a structure that wouldn't have seemed unusual one or two hundred years ago. There were plenty of windows to let in the natural light and allow a clear view of the surrounding forest, and she couldn't help her excitement at the thought of using the woodstove for the first time. The sound and smell of a crackling fire would be a welcome comfort. There was a rack with cut wood on the porch, but she didn't think it would last more than a few weeks. She'd have to chop more before long.

Sophie frowned; she wasn't eager to have to perform that sort of work just to meet her basic needs, and she hadn't really thought about it before moving out here. There hadn't been time. It would be a while before she adjusted to this place, to the lifestyle she'd chosen. But eventually, she would settle into normal. A *new* normal.

Because she'd arrived just ahead of the moving truck, she hadn't had a good look of the cabin. She walked around the right side, entering the chillier air in the building's shadow. The ground was a carpet of autumn colors, and small trees grew within twenty or thirty feet of the exterior wall. A few large, dark rocks jutted up from the fallen leaves, many sporting growths of green, fuzzy-looking moss.

The hairs on the back of her neck rose. Sophie slipped out her tongue to wet her suddenly dry lips and scanned the area.

This feeling—the feeling of being watched—had become uncomfortably familiar to her since she'd finally left Tyler. Recognizing her paranoia did little to limit its effects. She constantly expected Tyler to find her, to proclaim his love and promise everything would be better, to tell her how sorry he was and how he would be a better man for her, the man she deserved.

But Tyler's words were empty. They always had been and always would be. In his heart, Tyler believed he already *was* the man she deserved, because Sophie had always needed one thing above all else—to be put in her place. She was *his*, and that would never change. *He* would never change.

Her anxiety had only increased in the two weeks since he'd been released from jail. She'd had six months of freedom to get everything arranged so he couldn't find her when he got out. At the onset, that had seemed ample time, but once the legal processes had begun, she realized six months was *nothing*. Their divorce still wasn't finalized, and now he was free, and she knew he'd be looking for her. What good would the restraining order she had against him do? If he'd never been deterred by her begging, her tears, her bruises and blood, why would he be thwarted by a piece of paper?

The feeling of being watched persisted, but this was…*different*. It didn't seem to trigger the same panic she'd experienced all the other times. She brushed the sensation off. There was no one here but her; if she *was* being watched, it was probably by a wild animal cowering in a bush somewhere.

She made her way to the back of the house. The two rear windows belonged to the bathroom and the bedroom, and she noted that the former's wasn't the frosted glass to which she was accustomed; despite the remoteness of the property, she'd have to do something about that eventually. She continued around to the other side and cried out in excitement.

A small shelter stood against the wall beneath which were stacks and stacks of neatly piled wood. There had to be hundreds of pieces arranged here. It meant one less thing to worry about as she got her bearings here. The previous owner must've kept the wood stores well-stocked. From what Sophie's friend Kate said, the place had been used as a rental for hunters, seeing most of its usage during the fall and winter months.

Sophie took her cell out of her pocket and frowned. No signal. That drove home just how far away she was from the life she'd known; cell service was one of those things easily taken for granted until it was gone. She'd have to call Kate when she went into town to buy groceries the next day. Kate would want to know that Sophie had made it safe and sound.

Returning to her car, she popped the trunk and pulled out the suitcase she'd lived out of over the last couple weeks—she'd spent the time since Tyler's release in a hotel, waiting for Kate's purchase of the cabin to close. Sophie had moved as quick as possible once the sale was final, arranging the movers and utilities with Kate's help. The power had been turned on this morning, and her internet was supposed to be installed the next day, but it would be almost two weeks before the phone company could get someone out to activate her landline.

She'd make do with what she had for now. Closing the trunk, she went to the passenger door and opened the glove compartment, removing the holstered revolver from within. The gun was heavy now, heavier than it had ever seemed before, but it was a comforting weight.

I am not going to be a victim again.

Slipping the revolver into her other coat pocket, she walked to the porch and climbed the steps, rolling the suitcase behind her. The screen door's hinges creaked when she tugged it open. She held it ajar with her leg, grasped the knob of the interior door, and entered her home.

Outside, everything had smelled rich and alive, earthy and natural. The scent of wood was more refined within the cabin, and Sophie enjoyed the smell. It was calming and comforting; the perfect aroma for the place where she meant to recover.

To her left was the small kitchen area. A rough stone counter ran the length of the far wall, with distressed wood cabinets above and below it. Sunlight spilled in through the large window over the sink. The living room was to the right, part of the same open space as the kitchen. The wood stove rested in the farthest corner, set atop a stone platform with more stonework on the walls behind it. She'd set up her little desk at the side window that looked out into the forest, and her couch and TV were positioned so she could face the porch. She would rather have had the couch turned toward the stove to take advantage of its heat, but she couldn't take the thought of having her back to the door and all the windows at the same time.

Just the thought of it made her feel unsafe; she needed to have the outdoors—her *escape* route—in sight.

Her bookcase stood to the side of her desk, and there were cardboard boxes stacked along the wall between it and the woodstove. The boxes represented the majority of her worldly possessions apart from the furniture that had already been moved into place. It wouldn't take long to unpack, and she knew the house would still look somewhat bare when she was done. She hoped to remedy that in time. Once she settled in, she planned to visit some of the numerous antique shops and flea markets in the surrounding towns to find some knick-knacks and décor to give this cabin a lived-in feeling and make it her own.

Straight ahead were three doors—the bathroom on the left and her bedroom on the right with a linen closet in between. The cabin was small, but it was all she needed.

She went to the desk, placed her phone atop it, and deposited the revolver in the middle drawer. After shrugging off her coat, she draped it over the chair and walked into the bedroom.

The movers had already set up her bed—a simple metal frame with a wrought iron headboard, a box spring, and a queen mattress. The metal work had an intricate design; she'd known she had to have it the moment she saw it in the thrift store. There was no way she would've kept the bed she'd shared with Tyler. It carried too many memories.

Sophie took in another deep breath, closed her eyes, and released it slowly, pushing aside those dark recollections. "New home. New life. I got this."

Opening her eyes, she lifted her suitcase onto the bed and started unpacking. She hung a few garments in the closet, but most of her clothing went into the small, four-drawer dresser on the wall across from the foot of the bed. In her old house, she'd kept everything in a huge walk-in closet that had been brimming with colorful outfits and shoes. Now, she could fit all her clothes in one suitcase. She found that she missed neither the space nor the abundance of clothing. She'd kept only what she was comfortable in, just like it should've been all along.

She returned to the living room, found the box containing her bedding, made the bed, and unpacked the other boxes. She stored the toiletries, utensils, plates, and pots and pans in their new places. The nails scattered about on the walls served well enough for hanging the few framed pictures she possessed. She paused to examine one of the photos; it had been taken on Easter when Sophie was about ten years old. She was in a pastel green dress with white lace gloves and flats, flanked by her smiling parents. Her mom had done Sophie's hair that morning, curling it and pulling the spiraled strands up into a messy, beautiful bun. She'd always loved it when her mom styled her hair.

Eyes watering, she pressed a fingertip to the glass and brushed it over the images of her mother and father. It'd been six years since their deaths. Despite the time that had passed, she often found it hard to believe they were gone. She'd caught herself thinking about visiting them for Sunday dinner from time to time, just like she had every weekend since she'd moved out of their house for college. The reminder that they were gone, that there wouldn't be Sunday dinner with them ever again, always struck her hard.

With a soft, sad smile, Sophie turned away from the pictures.

Kneeling in front of her bookcase, she pulled the box of books closer and transferred them onto the shelves. Her collection was greatly diminished from its apex; Tyler had thrown away most of her books over the years, deeming them *trash*.

These were all she'd managed to save—a few of her favorites and the novels she'd written herself.

She touched the cover of one, tracing the bold white letters of her name—*Josephine Davis*. Tyler hadn't liked that she continued to use her maiden name for the little while she'd written after they were married.

She'd been forced to give up her dream for so long...

Her skin tingled, and the hair on her arms rose. Turning her head, Sophie looked out the front window. The forest was still and serene in the dwindling sunlight. She squinted, carefully studying everything in view, but couldn't discern either man or beast amidst the trees.

So why do I feel like someone is watching me again?

It was because of *him*. Tyler. He'd made her this way, had made Sophie fear her own damned shadow.

Holding the book to her chest, she squeezed it until her fingers ached. Why had she never allowed herself to be angry at him *before*? She wouldn't let him control her life any more. She was taking it back—taking *everything* back.

CRUCE REMAINED in the darkness beneath the canopy as he moved closer to the cabin. He flowed over the leaf-covered ground and whispered through the branches and stems of the undergrowth, gently rustling the vegetation. The surrounding shadows called to him; they begged him to release the sham of a shape into which he'd coalesced, to disperse himself, to lose himself in their soothing embrace and become one with them. As always, he shrugged off their call.

His hunger was stronger than the lure of unattainable oblivion.

The female mortal stood in the bedchamber, arranging her bedding. Cruce lingered just beyond the light spilling out through her window, unwilling to look away from the human. The familiar smells of his forest—rotting leaves, damp earth, a hundred different plants and trees—had been muted since he was cursed, but he'd clearly scented the human while she was outside earlier in the day. Lavender and vanilla. Her sweet perfume lingered in his senses, stirring his hunger further.

She looked and smelled *delicious.*

And the life force she emanated was maddening; he felt its strength even now, and he longed to sample it. He wanted to draw it into himself and fill the void that had been left inside by the fae queen's dark sorcery.

Though she was not the first mortal to come to this structure in the last few months, she was the first to stay for more than a few hours since last winter—the first to stay after sundown. When he'd sensed the intrusion in his woods, he'd expected to discover more of the hunters who often sheltered in this building. He'd expected another group of mortals seeking to take from his kingdom without giving *anything* in return, not even a small display of respect or thankfulness.

Days had passed since his last feeding, and Cruce had been ready to attack without provocation, damn the daylight. But then he'd scented *her,* and that flare of aroma on the otherwise scentless air had curtailed his ravenous fury.

Hidden in the deepening shadows beneath the trees while night approached, Cruce had watched as the mortal removed her belongings from the containers stacked inside. She'd paused several times to stare down at the objects in her hand as though in deep contemplation before resuming her work. When she emerged from within and collected chopped wood from the porch, it had taken all his willpower to keep from going to her.

He'd felt her life force throughout his vigil and had grown increasingly aware of the emotions tied to it as time passed—sorrow and fear, both delectable to feast upon. And yet they were underlaid by a deep resilience, and a burgeoning sense of *hope*.

Cruce moved closer still, avoiding the light cast from within the building. The mortal swept her hair back out of her face. Her skin looked so smooth and soft, so *warm*, and he longed to caress her with his own hands, but he would not be able to reclaim his physical form for nine more days, when the full moon rose on All Hallows Eve. Only then could he trail his fingertips over her pale flesh and share in her heat. Only then could he truly know her taste. Perhaps the timing of her arrival was more fortuitous than he'd first realized.

Were long dormant desires truly the cause of the pull he felt toward her? He hungered, yes, but this was more than mere hunger, more than lust. This was something new, and his instinct was to await the full moon to learn the truth of it.

Until then...

No. There was no sense in waiting, no sense in giving in to vague, mysterious feelings. He hungered *now*, and that hunger tore at him, bleeding into every wisp of his incorporeal being, demanding satisfaction. This mortal's life force would go a long way in quieting his hunger.

She stepped to the window and reached up to check the latch before grasping the curtains. Her lips were a healthy pink, her hair the same auburn as many of the autumn leaves over-head. She hesitated, her warm brown eyes—the most honest eyes he'd ever seen—falling upon him. For an instant, he felt connected to her and could almost see thin, silvery strands leading between them. Hunger roared within him, but it was a different sort of hunger, deeper and more consuming than his need for stolen life energies.

It was a hunger solely for *her*.

After a few moments, she shook her head, dropped her gaze, and pulled the curtains closed. The connection was immediately severed, and the emptiness within Cruce expanded to new depths. The interior light was reduced to a narrow line at the center of the window.

Leaving part of himself anchored in the shadows of the undergrowth, Cruce glided closer to the glass, stretching across the open ground. Through the slitted curtains, he saw the mortal walk to the far side of her bed. She crawled atop it, drew the blanket over herself, and reached for the lamp on a nearby stand.

There was a soft *click*, and the room was plunged into darkness.

She was entering her most vulnerable state—sleep. Not that humans were able to defend themselves against him, these days. They seemed to have lost their knowledge of the traditions and rituals that might once have afforded them some protection from beings such as Cruce.

Withdrawing from the window, he crept toward the front of the cabin. The forest's night sounds assailed him from all around; every living thing within his domain demanded his attention at once. Even the trees called to him. At the height of his power, the networks of tangled roots beneath the ground had served as a series of highways for him, and his magic had allowed him easy passage. Now he was reduced to stalking between the boughs like a shameful beast.

Long ago, he might've considered the wellbeing of his woods and the creatures dwelling within them.

These days, hunger seemed to consume his every thought.

He swept up to the side window and peered through. The interior lights were off, save for a relatively small, soft one in the kitchen. It cast deep shadows across the rest of the large room, providing a potential path with minimal exposure along the way. The light wouldn't do him any lasting harm, but it weakened him significantly, and he had no desire to feel weaker than the curse had already left him.

He continued forward, rounding the corner and flowing

through the porch railing. The female mortal's scent lingered here, a single point of clarity where all else was diminished and distant. Cruce paused to luxuriate in it. Now that he was closer, he detected the femininity of her aroma, and it stirred something within him that hadn't been awoken in ages.

Flattening himself against the wooden floorboards, he passed through the tiny gaps beneath the front doors. The air inside the cabin was noticeably warmer—for Cruce, that meant a slight shift toward more tolerable cold. There was no longer heat in his existence.

Cruce swept across the floor, veering away from the kitchen's glow. He passed through the shadows of her upholstered seating, unable to bring himself to study the objects around him because her smell was growing stronger, and he *yearned*, he *hungered*; he *needed* to have her.

Hunger outweighing caution, he crossed through the light and slipped through the open doorway into the mortal's bedchamber. He drew himself up, gathering the wisps of shadow that comprised him into a vaguely humanoid form.

The darkness of her room was welcoming. Starlight—as bright to him now as daylight once had been—flowed in through the slitted curtains. It gently draped her body, which was obscured beneath a blanket, in a silver glow. The paleness of her face was accentuated by her shimmering hair.

He moved closer to the bed. The mortal's life force pulsed from her, sweeping over him in a warm, consuming wave that made his shadows ripple. Her scent was more concentrated here, more alluring. Forming a hand from his darkness, he reached toward her. The faintest brush against her skin would give him a tantalizing sample of the sustenance she would provide.

Placing his hand atop the blanket, he focused his will on interacting with it. As a shade, he did not fully exist in either the physical world or the realm of spirits, making it difficult for him to interact with either plane. But the full moon of All Hallows Eve was near, and his ability to manipulate physical objects was strengthening with its approach. On that night, the veil between realms would be weakest, and his curse would afford him a physical form—a vulnerable, mortal body, divorced from the powers he'd once commanded.

Slowly, Cruce drew the blanket down the human's body. She stirred, rolling onto her side, and curled on herself as though seeking warmth or comfort. The crease between her delicate brows caught his attention; it seemed a troubled expression.

He had no reason to concern himself with the cares of mortals. At best, they'd been worshippers, making offerings and paying respects, but those days had long since passed. Now they were either potential threats to his forest or food—usually both. His dependence on them to satiate the worst of his hunger was infuriating and insulting, just as the queen had undoubtedly intended. But at least feeding on humans prevented him from taking from his forest and weakening himself in the long run.

As he swept his gaze over this small, vulnerable mortal, studying the way her bedclothes sculpted to her thighs and the curve of her backside, her scent permeated his very being. He shifted his hand to her pants and trailed it up her leg. The soft fabric was merely a suggestion of feeling beneath his fingers, a phantom sensation for a phantom hand, but the warm, yielding flesh under that layer of fabric was *real*. He felt it, felt *her*.

It was unlike anything he'd experienced since he was cursed.

Cruce moved his hand higher, thrumming with anticipation —but for what? For a taste of her life force, or a taste of *her*?

He withdrew his hand, reabsorbing it into his shadowy form. The heat he'd felt through her bedclothes spread through him for an instant—the first taste of warmth he'd had in nearly two decades. It gave way to familiar, numbing cold as it faded.

During the long years of his curse, he'd fed his hunger by draining the life from countless creatures—human and animal alike. Not once had contact with any of them produced such sensations. The rush of freshly consumed life force was a euphoria all its own, however fleeting, but this touch was too intriguing to dismiss outright.

He felt his form stretching and growing, rising to envelop the mortal and rip her life force from her chest, to greedily devour her essence. Something within him protested; this was not *right*.

The female moaned and turned onto her back, drawing a hand up to rest beside her head.

Cruce jerked himself backward, thinning against the wall. Hunger strained within him, pushing toward the mortal, drawn to her heat, her soft breath, her *life*, threatening to tear him asunder as it battled that sense of wrongness.

The mortal's scent eased over him again, eased *through* him, and he latched onto it.

He was not a slave to these urges any more than he was a slave to the fae queen. Cruce was master of these woods, lord of this forest, and he would not take this mortal. Not *yet*. She was too intriguing. After nearly two centuries of monotony in his damnation, she provided the first chance for change.

His curse was not broken, but if he could bypass some of its effects, even for a short while, it would be well worth the delay in devouring her essence. Once she no longer served as a worthwhile diversion, he could be rid of her. *After* All Hallows Eve.

With one final glance at her troubled face, Cruce withdrew from her home and darted deeper into the forest. Tonight, he'd have to feed upon one of the beasts he'd once protected to sate his hunger.

CHAPTER TWO

SOPHIE WOKE, shivering, to a beam of bright sunlight shining through the slit between the curtains. She was curled into a ball at the center of her bed, arms tucked close to her chest and hands fisted beneath her chin. Cool air kissed her exposed skin where her pajamas had ridden up. She sighed, closed her eyes, and reached down for the blanket. It wasn't there. Lifting her head, she opened her eyes and looked toward the foot of the bed.

One corner of the blanket lay at the edge of the mattress; the rest had fallen off the bed sometime before she'd woken.

Groaning, Sophie dropped her head onto her pillow and glanced at the clock. It was a quarter till nine. She stared at the glowing green numbers with some surprise. She couldn't remember the last time she'd slept past six.

She'd expected to sleep fitfully, to wake up randomly throughout the night. The routine had been drilled into her for years—get up early to set out Tyler's clothes, make coffee and breakfast, and ensure he had everything he needed to start his day. Though it had been six months since they'd lived together, she'd never been able to turn off the internal alarm that went off every morning, demanding she get up and get moving or suffer the consequences.

But for the first time in a long while, Sophie had slept deeply. Comfortably. Her body felt relaxed and refreshed, and embarrassingly, there was a faint pulse between her legs. She couldn't remember having any dreams, but she imagined they must have been good for once.

Despite feeling rejuvenated, she was *freezing*.

Sitting up, she slipped off the bed and slid her feet into her warm, fuzzy slippers. Making her way into the living room, Sophie grabbed her throw blanket, swung it over her shoulders, and pulled the sides closed over her chest.

She crouched in front of the woodstove and opened it. "No wonder it's so cold in here."

Picking up the fire poker, she stirred up the ashes, revealing the few embers still glowing within. The fire had nearly burned out during the night. She could only hope she'd have a good feel for how to keep it burning comfortably from dusk to dawn by the time winter set in. She added some newspaper and another log, lit the paper with a match, and waited to make sure the wood caught fire before closing the stove and heading into the kitchen to make coffee.

Not long after, she stepped out onto the porch with the blanket on her shoulders and a steaming mug cupped between her hands. The air was brisk, and the sheen of frost covering the fallen leaves gleamed in the golden morning light, sparkling like diamonds scattered across the ground. Sophie inhaled deeply and closed her eyes, relishing the fresh air.

Her skin tingled with the sudden sensation of being watched, and her heartbeat quickened. She scanned her surroundings, sweeping her gaze over trees and undergrowth, but just like the day before, she saw nothing out of the ordinary.

"Hello?" she called.

The only answer she received was her own echo.

Sophie released a long, slow breath and shook her head, running a hand through her mussed hair. "God, he screwed me up."

Shoving aside all thoughts of Tyler, she blew on her coffee and took a careful sip. She let herself enjoy the cool, bright morning, let herself soak in the beauty of nature. She'd lived in the city for her whole life until she'd moved to the suburbs with Tyler, and this was a welcome change from those manmade, manicured landscapes. This was the first place she'd been that felt *peaceful*.

Except I still feel like I'm not alone.

Clenching the edges of the blanket together with one hand, Sophie peered over the rim of her mug to search the trees again before turning around and going back inside.

After getting dressed and brushing her hair and teeth, Sophie took a trip to town—a twenty-minute drive through winding backroads that cut through lush forest and green hills. The town itself, Raglan, was small, with gorgeous, old-fashioned homes lining the main road. Pots of orange and yellow mums hung from the light posts along the sidewalks, and pumpkins, ghosts, skeletons, and witches decorated the lawns and windows of many of the houses.

Sophie smiled. With everything that was going on, she'd forgotten how close Halloween was. It had been her favorite holiday as a child, and she still loved it as an adult. She loved seeing all the costumes as kids ran from door to door trick-or-treating. In years past, she'd bought boxes of full-sized candy bars, decorated her house, and even worn her own costumes as she waited for the neighborhood kids to show up. The weeks prior to Halloween used to mean horror movie marathons and trips to Halloween stores just to look around in delight.

Her smile fell. That's how it had been until Tyler decided he didn't want his wife *displaying herself to all the local teenagers*.

She shook her head; she wasn't under his control anymore.

Turning into the parking lot of the local grocery store, she found a spot and cut the engine. She grabbed her purse and dug her phone out. Her brows rose; seven missed calls and fourteen messages. Sophie chuckled and skimmed through the text messages—all from Kate.

How was the drive?
Are you getting settled in? I want pictures!
Why haven't you called or texted? Getting worried here.
Sophie, ANSWER YOUR PHONE!

"OH, KATE." Sophie smiled, pressed the call button, and lifted the phone to her ear.

The first ring was cut short by a familiar voice. "It's about damn time! Where have you been?" Kate demanded. "I've been trying to get a hold of you since yesterday! You can't do that to me!"

"I know! I'm sorry! I would've called you, but there's no cell reception at the cabin. I'm in the grocery store parking lot right now."

"What about Facetime?"

"I'm getting the internet installed this afternoon."

"Good." Kate sighed. "Sorry, Sophie. I was worried."

"I know. I didn't mean to make you worry." Sophie tightened her grip on the phone. "Is he…?"

There was a sound on the other end, as though Kate was pulling down the blinds. Sophie could just imagine her peeking through the slits to look across the street. "He's still at the house. I've been keeping an eye on him."

Sophie released a soft, relieved breath. Kate lived directly across from the house Sophie and Tyler had shared, and she'd been Sophie's secret friend while Tyler was at work. It had been difficult in the beginning; Sophie hadn't wanted anyone to know what went on between her and Tyler. She'd pretended not to know Kate—beyond being the woman from across the street —when he was around, which had involved playing dumb at the supermarket from time to time.

But Kate was a smart, compassionate woman. She'd picked up on the signs, and she'd noticed Sophie's bruises. The first few times, it had been easy to play them off as the results of accidents; Sophie claimed clumsiness, her lack of coordination hadn't been a lie. But before long, Kate's perceptiveness became too much, and Sophie had admitted the truth. She'd begged Kate not to say a word. She didn't know what Tyler would do to her or Kate if word got out.

Kate had agreed with extreme reluctance, under the condition that she and Sophie work together on a plan to get her out of the relationship safely. Even then, Sophie hadn't believed there *could* be a safe exit from her marriage. But they'd kept up the friendly neighbor act, kept outwardly pretending everything was all right, everything was normal.

And Kate had kept her word. Their plans to get Sophie out hadn't made a difference, in the end, but Kate's friendship was what saved Sophie.

Kate's guilt for holding her silence and not acting sooner was immense, but Sophie had made it clear in the time since— she owed her *life* to Kate. They'd been working together ever since to take all the necessary legal action and make sure Tyler never found Sophie again.

"What's he been doing?" Sophie asked.

"I'm...not sure. He's still angry. I heard him shouting the other day, and he took a bunch of trash out to the curb on garbage day this week. I think a lot of it was stuff you left behind, because he dragged most of it back inside right before the truck came. I think he's obsessing. *Bad.*"

Sophie closed her eyes and leaned her head back against the headrest. "Thank you, Kate. For everything."

"Of course. I just want you safe. And once everything has settled and your divorce is official, I'm coming to visit! I could use a little country air."

Sophie smiled. "It's beautiful out here. There are so many colors."

"It's a date then."

They spoke for a little longer before Sophie ended the call, promising to Facetime her later.

She got out of the car, locked it, and walked into the grocery store.

Several people watched her as she entered the building. Sophie offered a timid smile to one of them, an older woman who was working a check stand, and grabbed a cart. It didn't take her long to get what she needed—she wanted to keep things simple, which meant a lot of soup and sandwiches for the next few weeks. After stopping to pick out a birthday card for Kate, she headed up to the check lanes. The store was smaller than she was used to, and the prices were higher, but she didn't care. The move already felt worth it.

"You're a new face," said the elderly cashier as Sophie placed her items on the conveyer belt.

"I just moved here yesterday," Sophie replied, glancing at the woman's nametag. Doris.

"It's so wonderful to see fresh faces in our little town. And yours it such a pretty one." The register beeped as Doris scanned Sophie's groceries.

Sophie smiled, cheeks warming. "Thank you."

"Did you buy the yellow two-story down the street? Gorgeous flowers."

Sophie shook her head. "No. I'm in a log cabin off the old highway, about twenty minutes outside town."

"That ole hunting lodge?" Doris's hand paused, and she

frowned, her eyes moving over Sophie. "A young lady like you shouldn't be out there all by yourself."

"I'm fine. I actually...really like it. It's a nice change from the city."

"Well, just be careful." She placed the final item in the bag. "I could send my Ron out to check on you from time to time, if you'd like. That old bugger needs something more to do besides pinching my behind."

Sophie chuckled and shook her head. "No, it's all right. I'm fine, really. But thank you."

Doris rang up the total and wished Sophie a wonderful day after she passed over the receipt.

While loading her bags into the car, Sophie paused. She felt...lighter. It was strange to realize that she actually *could* have a good day without fear of consequences.

Time. That's all I need.

Sophie watched the words race across the screen as her fingers flew over the laptop's keys. The story was pouring out of her; each scene played vividly in her mind, and she wrote as fast as she could to preserve all the details. She stopped occasionally to refill her iced tea or admire the view of the woods through the window.

It took her a while to realize she was enjoying herself. She was writing, and during that time, she was free of worry, free of fear; she was just...being herself.

Even the lingering feeling of being watched, the presence she swore was hovering somewhere nearby, couldn't diminish her elation.

Whether it was a result of an overactive imagination, her paranoia, or both, she swore something was there with her. She wanted to believe it was a kind entity, this ghost, or spirit, or whatever it was, that it was there to watch over and protect her.

She didn't want to think about the alternatives.

A knock at the front door made her jump. It was so sudden, so unexpected, that her heart leapt into her throat. She stood up and stumbled backward, nearly knocking over her chair. Panting, she clutched the fabric of her shirt and pressed herself back against the bookcase as though she could shrink into it. Her chest ached, her heart was racing, and she couldn't breathe; terror had taken over.

No! He's not here. He hasn't found me. I'm safe. Safe. Safe...

Sophie closed her eyes and forced herself to breathe slow and deep, hoping to curtail the frantic beating of her heart.

"He's not here. He's not here," she whispered to herself over and over. "I'm safe. He's not here."

Tears stung her eyes. She shifted to the desk and lowered her hand to the middle drawer; she knew how to use the revolver, and that knowledge lent her some strength.

The knock repeated, louder and more insistent than before.

"Who is it?" she called, proud that her voice didn't crack.

"My name is Dan," said a man from outside. His voice was nothing like Tyler's. "I'm from Sky Link Telecommunications, here to install your internet."

Sophie released another shaky breath and brushed the moisture from her eyes. Her limbs were weak and trembling as she walked to the window and peered out to see the white and blue van in the driveway with *SKY LINK* on the side in big letters. That eased her some, but not entirely. Tyler was cunning, and determined, and when he wanted something...

She unlocked the front door and opened it a crack. Looking up, she met brown eyes. Brown. Not blue. *Dan*, not Tyler.

"Sorry," she muttered and took a step back, opening the door wider.

"No problem," he said with a smile. He hesitated as he opened the screen door. "You okay?"

"Yeah," Sophie replied. "Just a...little lightheaded."

Dan frowned. "Do you have a certain spot you want it set up?"

"I'm all wireless, so anywhere is fine."

"All right. I'll take a look around and see what we have to work with then I'll be out of your hair."

"Thank you"

The technician was a tall man, and though he seemed friendly, Sophie couldn't help her unease at being alone with him. Leaving the front door open wide, she moved back to the desk and kept out of his way as he worked, drawing comfort from the gun in the nearby drawer. She felt horrible about it— Dan was just trying to do his job—but she couldn't shake her fear. It didn't matter how many times she told herself it was ridiculous; the damaged had been done. Tyler had made her this way, and she hated him for it.

Dan worked swiftly and kept to himself, focusing on his task. Once her internet was up and running, he had her sign the work order on his tablet, bid her a good afternoon, and left.

After the front door was closed and locked, Sophie leaned her back against it, struggling for calm. Anger and shame swirled inside her. She wanted her confidence, her courage, and her security back. She just wanted to be *normal*. But Tyler had stripped away the person she'd been one day at a time. In the grand scheme of things, five years didn't seem like so long, but it had been a living hell for Sophie. Six months hadn't been enough to heal her internal wounds—especially when the first few weeks of it had been spent in the hospital, recovering from the beating Tyler had given her.

Pushing away from the door, she stepped into the kitchen and threw together a ham sandwich, pairing it with chips and a bottled water. She carried her simple dinner to her desk and ate slowly as she wrote, managing a few hundred more words before calling it quits for the night.

She looked out the window. The sky outside was lit only by a faint orange glow. It'd be full dark soon, and she still needed to call Kate.

After cleaning her dishes, she took a quick shower, pulled on some soft, cozy pajamas—complete with oversized, fluffy socks—and sat down at her desk again. She opened the Facetime app and clicked on her only contact. She was brushing her damp hair when Kate accepted the call.

Kate's wide, green eyes and infectious smile instantly filled Sophie with warmth.

"Hi!" Kate exclaimed, waving. "Looks like *someone* just took a shower."

Sophie smiled. "Yeah."

"So, you had someone out to install your internet, hmm? Was he hot?"

Sophie's hand stilled.

Kate leaned closer to the camera, smile faltering. "Soph, what's wrong?"

Sophie shook her head and set the brush down on the desk. "It's nothing. Just..."

Movement in the corner caught her attention. She snapped her head to the side, eyes darting back and forth, but there was nothing there. A chill ran up her spine; she could've sworn she'd seen *something*.

"Sophie?" Kate urged.

"It's nothing," Sophie repeated, more to herself than to Kate. She slowly faced her friend again.

"You had an anxiety attack, didn't you?"

"I...almost, yeah," Sophie replied. "I guess I just wasn't expecting the installer. Well, I was, but I was distracted, and he startled me, and all I could think of was...Tyler. That he'd found me. That he was *here*."

"He's not, sweetie. He's still here, across the street, in your old house. Hundreds of miles away."

"I know that, Kate. That's what makes this worse. He's not even here and he still has so much control over me. I can't get away from him. He's always *here*, in my head." Her eyes stung, and her vision blurred with tears.

"Aww, Sophie. It will get better with time. I *promise*. I will do everything I can to make sure he never touches you again."

It didn't matter that she'd only met Kate a few years ago; Sophie felt like she'd known her forever. She was a sister, a confidant, a guardian angel. "I love you."

"I love you, too." Kate smiled. "Go get some rest. We'll talk again soon."

"Good night, Kate."

"Night, sweetie."

Sophie disconnected the call and leaned back, settling her heels on the edge of her chair and drawing her legs to her chest to lean her chin atop them. She stared out the window, past her reflection, to the shadows outside. She stayed like that for a long while. Exhaustion—mostly mental—had caught up to her, but she wasn't ready to go to bed for fear that she'd see Tyler in her sleep, as she so often did.

The nearby presence hadn't diminished, but she found a strange degree of comfort in it now. Logic told her it wasn't real; there was no one outside, no one in the house, no one *here*. She was by herself. It was likely that overly imaginative part of her mind seeking out a substitute guardian angel while she was so far away from her real-life hero, Kate.

With a soft sigh, she unfolded her legs and rose. She added a couple logs to the woodstove, arranging them with the poker to give new life to the fire, and closed her eyes to savor the warmth before closing the door. She went about her new nighttime routine—she turned off her computer, checked the locks on all the windows and doors, and went into the bathroom to brush her teeth and relieve herself.

Sophie looked in the mirror and tilted her head. It wasn't the battered wife of the last few years staring back at her, but it also wasn't the carefree young writer she'd been before Tyler. She was at a crossroads. Though her body was no longer a tapestry of bruises and split lips, she would always carry scars upon her soul. But she had a chance to define what those scars would mean going forward.

She entered her bedroom, pulled the covers back, and climbed into bed. Reaching over, she shut off the lamp. The soft nighttime glow from outside bathed her room in gentle silver. She stared up at the dark ceiling after pulling up the blanket.

"Please don't let him find me."

CRUCE FORMED himself in the corner, drawing the ethereal tendrils that comprised him into the pathetic shadow of a body. The mortal on the bed, Sophie, had closed her eyes, but her breathing suggested she was not yet asleep. Her features were strained, and the last words she'd spoken had carried a desperate tone. After overhearing her conversation with Kate through the strange, magical device on her desk, he knew that Sophie was haunted by something.

By *someone.*

His urge to shelter her from her emotions was an unfamiliar one; Sophie's distress had created tension within him that he'd not felt since before his damnation, and he'd wanted nothing more than to soothe her. Seeing her in such a state had brought him no pleasure.

And yet her past, her traumas, were meaningless to Cruce. Her life was measured in the space between his heartbeats—or would've been, had he a physical heart. *Tyler* had done her harm at some point, but these humans should've been nothing to Cruce but potential sustenance.

He eased closer to the bed. Outside, leaves rustled in the autumn wind, and the boughs of ancient trees creaked and moaned, but in here there was only the crackling of the fire from the next room and the gentle sound of this mortal's soft breath. It would take but a few moments to steal that breath from her forever. Given her state, would that not be a mercy?

Just as he might've ended the suffering of an injured hare, he could eliminate this human's fears and anxiety, could grant her eternal peace.

Even now, wisps of shadow extended toward her, hungry and probing, seeking out flesh through which to drink her essence. As much as he loathed his need to steal life from earthly creatures—leaving behind meat and bones to rot away— he could not deny its thrill. It provided him some of the only pleasure he'd known during his years as a cursed *thing*, however fleeting or shameful that pleasure proved.

He yanked back those tendrils abruptly. He'd not yet had his taste of her. He'd not yet felt her skin with his own fingers, had not yet drawn in her scent with his own nostrils or sampled her flavor with his own tongue. Until he came to know that physical contact with her, she was worth keeping alive.

At that moment, he found himself longing for her warmth far more than for the sustenance of her life force.

He sank down beside her bed, lowering his viewpoint to her level. She lay on her side, facing the wall behind him. Her breathing slowed and evened out gradually. For a long while, Cruce remained still, watching as her expression drifted between serenity and distress. Was she so troubled that even sleep could not grant relief from whatever burdens she carried during her waking hours?

Despite the occasional worry straining her features, she was beautiful.

Hers was not the beauty of the fae or the other ethereal beings that dwelled beyond the veil between worlds; hers was the beauty of mortality. She wore her struggles and triumphs, and her imperfections only sharpened her allure. Sophie possessed no glamour or magic to hide behind. She didn't have the cold, graceful sensuality of the fae queen or the raw sexual allure of a nymph. She was human. Short-lived, fragile, and oddly unique.

Moving carefully, he peeled the blanket off her body. The demands of his forest vied for his attention, but he had none to spare. His focus was solely upon Sophie.

She wore the same type of bedclothes she had the night before, and her position pulled the fabric taut over certain parts of her body—her backside and her small, rounded breasts primarily. Were it not so likely to wake her, he'd find it worth the effort to strip her clothing, to give himself direct access to her pale skin.

Cruce extended a tendril of shadow and trailed it along her outer thigh, moving it steadily higher. The same heat he'd felt the night before flowed into him, chasing away some of the eternal cold. Again, the fabric of her pants felt far-off, more like a memory than a current experience. But the *heat*! Sophie's warmth radiated beneath his touch, inviting him to move his shadowy limb higher. He gave in to the urge, sliding the tendril up to hook the hem of her shirt, brushing the waistband of her pants.

Sophie shifted and released a soft whimper. Her movements tugged her shirt slightly upward, exposing a strip of pale skin around her waist. Cruce lifted the shirt a little further, careful not to touch her skin directly.

There would be no turning back from this. If he touched her now, he would taste her life force—the life force that had teased him, maddened him, and called to him since her arrival. Despite his control up to this point, he wasn't sure if he'd be able to resist his hunger after touching Sophie.

Shaping the tendril into a hand, he lowered it onto Sophie's skin.

Fire blazed through Cruce, spreading across his shadows, devouring them; thrilling, tantalizing, and painful. For an instant, he lost control of his shape. His form swelled and dispersed throughout the room. Jolts of energy crackled within him, and Sophie's sweetness—her taste and scent—permeated him.

The sensations were overwhelming. His mind, which had comprehended the complex networks of plants and roots throughout the entirety of his forest, which had been connected to the thoughts of thousands upon thousands of the creatures that called these woods home, which had perceived the webs of magic running through all existence, was temporarily dominated by this mortal—and she was a mystery beyond his understanding. She consumed him, flooding him with emotions and imaginings he could scarcely piece together. Sophie left room for *nothing* inside Cruce but herself. Had he breath, it would have been stolen; had he a heart, it would have ceased beating.

She moaned appreciatively and nuzzled her face into her pillow.

Cruce withdrew and shuddered back from her, mind spinning. Icy cold flowed into him in the absence of contact between them, but its familiarity brought no clarity—instead, it only increased his want for her, his *need*.

Lingering pleasure rippled through him as he drew back the wisps of darkness that had been drifting across the room. He gathered himself into a tight bundle. Her scent remained with him, and her warmth seemed to pulse from the bed, just strong enough to keep his desire burning. He needed *more*—not of her essence, but of *her*.

All Hallows Eve could not arrive soon enough.

He departed from her home and sped into the forest to feed; he would control his hunger over the next week, would ensure he was in a state in which he could protect her. And, when the full moon restored his physical form, he would take Sophie as his own.

CHAPTER THREE

SOPHIE MOANED. *The soft, breathy sound was muted by the mist around her. Lust consumed her, dominating her senses and thoughts as a shadowy caress drifted over her body. There were no hands, only the illusion of them, their gentle touch sending tingles across her skin and heightening her desire.*

A shadow loomed over her, dark and powerful but not threatening. It exuded raw sensuality rather than menace. The shadow parted her thighs, and Sophie gasped as it swept a dark tendril over her exposed sex, its touch cool against her heated skin. The darkness stroked her; its wisps ran across her entire body, curling around her breasts to tease her nipples, filling her with its essence. Liquid heat flooded her. She cried out between panting breaths, arching her back as pleasure blazed through her.

"Please," she begged, reaching her hand out. Her fingers passed through the insubstantial form. Tendrils of shadow swirled around her wrist and flowed up her arm, leaving thrills in their wake. The shadows sank into her, became her, engulfed her, and she screamed with the force of the climax that overtook her.

Sophie was startled awake by her own sharp cry. Breathing raggedly, she sat up and placed a hand over her racing heart. She was hot—*too* hot—despite the chill of the air against her flushed cheeks. Her body buzzed with arousal. Her skin was warm and so sensitive that even her super-soft pajamas were irritating and stifling.

And worse…she'd come. *In her sleep.* She could feel the moisture between her thighs, soaking her underwear. Her body thrummed, and her sex still pulsed with the aftermath.

"Wow," she rasped, pressing a hand to her face as she caught her breath.

She'd had dreams of sex before, but this was wholly different; she rarely dreamed with such intensity. This had felt *real*. She tried to recall the details, but all she could remember were shadows, mist, and immense pleasure.

Gingerly, Sophie maneuvered to the edge of the bed and slipped off. She bit her lower lip to suppress a grin.

"What a way to start the morning." She chuckled.

Her blankets were already on the floor—she must've kicked them off in her sleep again—so she stripped the remaining bedding, including the mattress cover, and dumped them in the washing machine in the bathroom.

She paused while lowering the lid and returned it to the upright position. Hurriedly, Sophie pushed down her pajama pants and panties, pulled her shirt off over her head, and tossed them all into the washer. She shivered, her skin pebbling with the cold as she added detergent and set the dials. But her skin prickled with something more—awareness. She stilled, her chest suddenly tight, convinced there was someone—or something—behind her. Steeling herself, she glanced over her shoulder.

There was nothing there but her flower-patterned shower curtain.

Shaking her head, she pulled open the shower curtain—*still* nothing there—and started the water. It seemed to take forever to get hot.

After she'd showered and dressed, she built up the fire and made breakfast. The interior of the cabin was lit with a golden glow by the morning sunlight streaming in through the windows. How had this place looked when it was first built? Had the wood shined, or had it always possessed this distressed, rustic aesthetic?

She settled her throw blanket over her shoulders and stepped onto the porch to take in the crisp morning air. The more time she spent here, the more she was coming to love it. She could envision the exact place outside where she'd set up her worktable in the spring. It would sit in a shady spot facing the woods, surrounded by the sounds of nature; the perfect spot to get some writing done.

Sophie smiled. She was already planning for the future, making this place her home. That was a good sign.

She went back inside, grabbed her laptop, and settled on the sofa to write. The day flew by; even though she knew each minute was neither longer nor shorter than the last, they seemed to tick away faster and faster. The presence she'd felt since that morning remained a constant, and the sensation grew steadily stronger through the day. It was enough of a distraction to break her concentration by the evening.

With a sigh, she saved her work, closed the program, and set the computer aside. She tipped her head back and stared up at the ceiling.

Why had she been so skittish when the internet tech had come but retained her calm while this *presence* lingered around her at all hours? Something lurked within her home, something unseen, unknown, *impossible*. Ghosts, entities, phantoms, spirits…none of that was real. Was that why she felt no fear? After her time with Tyler, she knew all too well that the real world hurt a hell of a lot more than the imaginary one. The only real monsters were humans, and it was the face of one of those humans that haunted her every day.

She closed her eyes. She'd been incorrect; when left unchecked, her imagination *could* do quite a bit of damage. Whenever she heard a sound outside, whenever she saw a shadow move from the corner of her eye, she envisioned Tyler. The effects of those imaginings lingered for a long while after they occurred. She was just glad she hadn't dreamed of him since she'd moved in.

A puff of air brushed against the side of her neck and teased the loose strands of her hair. But it was too focused, too concentrated, to have been a breeze—and all the windows were closed.

Sophie sucked in a sharp breath, opened her eyes, and raised her head. A dark form moved at the edge of her vision. She swung her head to the side to follow its movement, but the shape vanished before she could get a good look at it.

Fear stole the breath from her lungs as she leapt off the couch and crossed the short distance to her desk. Her laptop slid onto the floor behind her, but she ignored it. Yanking open the middle drawer, she grabbed the gun, tore it out of its holster, and twisted to aim it toward the bedroom. That was where the shadow had gone.

Despite her two-handed grip, the revolver trembled.

"Who's there?" she demanded. Her heart pounded, echoing thunderously in her ears.

There was no answer, no sound at all except for her ragged breathing. Her chest constricted. She was on the verge of a panic attack.

She swept her gaze over the dimly lit room. Nothing moved.

Her laptop was face down on the floor, the light from its screen shining on the carpet. Sophie approached it cautiously, crouching nearby and reaching out blindly to take a hold of it. She kept her attention on the doorway to her bedroom.

Easing onto the floor, she settled the computer on her lap and risked looking at the screen only long enough to call Kate on Facetime. Sophie took a deep breath and held it as she counted the rings, silently praying for her friend to accept the call.

Just when she was convinced there would be no answer, the screen changed, and Kate's face appeared.

"Soph—"

"Where is he?" Sophie asked.

"Tyler? He's home. His car is sitting in the driveway." Kate frowned deeply. "Why?"

Sophie squeezed her eyes shut. When she opened them, dark blotches lingered in her vision for several seconds, but no shadows remained after they faded. The room was the same as it had been a moment before.

"Sophie, what's going on?"

Sophie was going insane. She was unstable, paranoid, suffering hallucinations, unable to cope on her own. Things had been great with Kate, but by herself, Sophie was...broken.

"You're scaring me, Soph. What's wrong?" Kate asked, voice rising.

"Nothing," Sophie said softly. She shook her head and lowered the gun. It was outside the camera's field of view, so her friend would never see it. "A bad dream, I think. I thought..."

"You're safe, sweetie. He's still here."

Sophie nodded.

"You okay?" Kate asked.

"Yeah. I just...need a little time to calm down. Thank you, Kate."

"Call me if you need me. Anytime."

"Love you."

"Love you, too."

Sophie closed the laptop, set it aside, and stood up. She scanned the room again before making a sweep of the entire house, checking every lock, every room, even the closets and cabinets. It was extreme, but it helped put her at ease.

Closing her eyes, Sophie took a deep, calming breath. "I dozed off," she said. "My eyes were tired, and I dozed off for a second. It was just one of those half-awake, half-asleep things."

Walking to the desk, she holstered the revolver and returned it to the drawer. She stood there for a time, leaning her hands on the edge of the desk, replaying Kate's words in her mind. Tyler was *there*, not *here*. Sophie was safe.

Lifting her head, Sophie looked out the window. The sky was awash with color, the clouds overhead painted in vibrant reds and golds with the approaching sunset.

Maybe it was cabin fever. She'd been cooped up in a hotel room for weeks, and even though this cabin was in the middle of the woods, she'd done little to enjoy her surroundings since her arrival. A walk would do her good. It was still light enough for a little easy exploration. She could get some exercise, clear her head, and be home before dark. Then she'd pretend none of this had happened. It had just been her mind playing tricks on her.

She put on her shoes, a sweater, and a long scarf before stepping outside. She jumped when the screen door slammed shut behind her.

"I've got to get that adjusted," she muttered, shoving her hands into her pockets as she started toward the woods. She'd have to look up some internet videos on how to change the tension on the self-closing hinges.

There was a faint trail off one side of the driveway; she assumed it had been used by the hunters who'd often rented the cabin. Months of disuse had left it strewn with broken branches and overgrown with vegetation. She set out along the path, twigs snapping and leaves crunching beneath her sneakers as she walked. The trees here were tall and thin, their lower trunks mostly bare of branches. The sporadic beams of sunlight breaking through the canopy cast a glittering, golden glow on the forest floor. Sophie extended a hand and brushed her fingers over the rough bark of a tree as she passed.

Her mind wandered with little provocation; she pretended she was in a whole new world and immersed herself in absorbing the beauty all around her.

She realized abruptly that the sunlight was gone, and the forest was cast in gloomy twilight—she'd lost track of time while her head was in the clouds.

"It's okay. I'll just head back." She stopped and turned around. "Just have to retrace my steps and I'll be home. I didn't walk far… Right?"

But she couldn't see a path on the forest floor anymore; she couldn't be sure of whether she'd wandered off it or it was simply so overgrown out here that it blended into the rest of the forest floor in the dimness. She had no idea how long she'd been walking.

Sophie was lost, and it was only getting darker with each passing moment.

Her heart thundered, cold perspiration beaded on her brow, and her lower lip trembled. The temperature was rapidly falling now that the sun had set, and her only warm clothing was a knitted sweater and a scarf.

"God, I am so stupid." She laughed at herself. "Seems to be my lot in life. Poor choices all around." She swept her gaze over her surroundings, searching for something—*anything*—that looked familiar, but nothing stood out.

"It's this way," she said with far more confidence than she felt. She walked in the direction she was facing. It took a few minutes for her to realize she was crying; silent tears streamed down her cheeks, leaving trails of cool moisture in their wake. She wiped at them with the backs of her hands.

She drew in a deep breath, seeking calm. "I got this. I'll figure this out. The trees have to end somewhere, right?" She paused for a moment, then snickered to herself. "God, if this was a book, readers would be calling me too stupid to live.

"But that's life, isn't it? We're human. We make mistakes—some of us more than others, and *boy* have I made more than my share. But we learn from them." There was no way in hell she'd ever trust a man like Tyler again, that was for damn sure. "Next time I decide to take an evening stroll, I'll leave breadcrumbs, or string, or...something."

There was a huff of breath accompanied by the snapping of a branch to her right. Sophie stilled. Ever so slowly, she turned to face the noise.

Not thirty feet away was an enormous black bear.

She nearly tripped over her own feet as she started, her heart leaping into her throat.

The bear lifted its head and stared at her.

Sophie raised her hands, palms out, and took a step back. "Nice bear. You just stay right there."

It huffed, scraped its giant paw across the ground, and opened its maw to release a roar.

Sophie whimpered and retreated several more steps. Why hadn't she brought the gun with her? Maybe it wasn't enough to down a bear, but it would've been *something*. "Please don't kill me. Oh, please don't. I don't taste good, I swear."

She struggled to recall a dozen articles she'd read on dealing with bears, but the information was too jumbled to extract, like gathered debris blocking the flow of a river.

The bear advanced.

Sophie turned around and hauled ass away from the beast, knowing even as she ran that it was the wrong thing to do. She might've screamed, but she was oblivious to everything but her impending demise. Her feet pounded on the forest floor as she wove through trees and leapt over fallen logs. The heavy, snarling breath of the bear alerted her to just how close behind it was. She *knew* humans couldn't outrun bears. All the same, she hadn't realized just how fast the big creatures were; the bear was quickly gaining on her.

She took a sharp left, bumping her shoulder into a tree, but she used the dull pain as fuel to push forward. She couldn't stop, couldn't slow.

The bear roared again. Sophie glanced over her shoulder; it was immediately apparent that it had been the *wrong* thing to do. Her foot struck something solid, and her upper half lurched forward. Crying out, she threw her hands forward just before she slammed into the ground. The breath burst from her lungs.

She rolled herself over as the bear caught up with her. She tried to scream, but she hadn't yet caught her breath.

Pain exploded in her side as the bear smacked her with a huge front paw, sending her tumbling several feet away. She groaned as she clawed and kicked onto her hands and knees. She wouldn't let herself die here, she *couldn't*. The will to fight, to *survive*, was buried within her, she just had to draw upon it. Sophie hadn't escaped one beast just to be killed by another.

Turning toward the bear, she drew upon all the willpower she had left and screamed as loudly as she could. The animal's approach faltered. It took a step back before rearing up on its hind legs, roaring as though to answer her challenge.

Something moved at the edge of her vision. Fearing another bear, Sophie shifted her gaze to the side. A large, dark shape darted by, turning sharply toward her. The temperature took a sudden drop as the shape approached.

The bear's call gained an uncertain note that quickly shifted to fear as the huge, shadowy *thing* charged. The black figure flared out impossibly wide, blocking Sophie's view of the bear completely. The thing was too dark for her to make details of hide, fur, or skin; it was so dark that she couldn't make out *any* details. Shadows seemed to bleed from the edges of its form to dissipate into the twilight.

The black thing quickly snapped itself closed, enveloping the bear completely. It reminded her of an octopus catching a fish in the net of its tentacles, but her mind—whether due to fear or lack of knowledge—couldn't identify any land creature that hunted in such a fashion, especially not anything so big.

The bear's sounds changed tone again, going from fearful to agonized. A chill ran through Sophie's bones; the calls were so full of suffering that she couldn't help but identify with them on some primal level. Her *soul* had made such sounds on her last night with Tyler.

She watched, frozen in terror, as the mass of darkness sank to the ground, and the bear's sounds dwindled until the woods were silent save for Sophie's panting breaths.

The shadows moved, rising like wisps of smoke from the motionless animal. The unnatural sight was enough to jar her out of her stupor.

Nope. Not happening.

Sophie's fingers dug ruts in the ground as she shoved herself to her feet. She turned and ran. She didn't know where she was going, didn't care, so long as she got away from *that*. Her side ached and throbbed, her throat was raw, and her lungs burned.

When she felt like she could go no farther, Sophie ducked behind a tree and pressed her back flat against the trunk. She closed her eyes. Her chest felt ready to burst and her legs were on fire with exertion.

Please don't find me. Please. Oh God, please don't.

She struggled to quiet her breathing even as she sucked in great lungfuls of air to recover from her panicked flight. The remembered image of the shadowy entity rising off the bear forced a scream into her throat. Biting her lips to contain her cries, she strained to listen for sounds of the *thing* approaching. She pressed her nails into the bark behind her.

"You need not flee," a voice—deep and resonating, at once like the guttural growling of the bear and the soft sighing of leaves in the wind—said from somewhere nearby.

Sophie gasped, eyes opening wide. A man? But she'd seen...
What *had* she seen?

*Crazy. I'm going crazy. That voice doesn't belong to a man; no
person could sound like that.*

This is all in my head.

Movement drew her attention to the space between two of
the trees ahead; the darkness shifted subtly and seemed to
deepen.

"You are safe, mortal."

Mortal?

Sophie closed her eyes again. "This is a dream. This *isn't* real.
I'm dreaming. There's no talking shadow, there was no...no
bear."

"Denial," the voice said, closer than before. Something
brushed over the leg of her pants, sending a whisper of cold
through to the flesh beneath.

She whimpered and leapt away from the tree, nearly falling
on her ass in the process, before turning to face the voice. As
twilight gave way to full night, everything but the deep gray of
the sky was black; she couldn't see whatever was talking
to her.

"Fear is survival," the voice said, drawing her attention
toward a fallen tree. A deeper shadow moved in the darkness,
long and sleek, giving her the impression of a huge wolf or
some sort of great cat—a panther, or a tiger. "But it will do you
no good now. I will not harm you, Sophie."

She reached up and clutched a handful of her sweater's
material over her chest. It was hard to breathe, to focus, while
her body was suffused with terror. "What...are you?"

The thing moved again and was briefly silhouetted against
the lighter sky; it seemed to be in the shape of a stag or an elk
for an instant. Then its body changed, rising taller, into something almost humanoid—though the massive antlers remained
in place—before melding into the shadows again.

"The spirit of this forest," it replied. "Guardian and ruler. This is *my* domain."

"W-What do you want?" She couldn't stop trembling.

The voice came from immediately behind her. "To protect what is mine."

Sophie spun around, searching with wide eyes for the deeper shadow, but she couldn't distinguish it from the other darkness.

The icy touch slid across her back, from shoulder blade to shoulder blade. A chill ran down her spine, making her shudder, but an unexpected spark of desire flared with it. Where had she felt that touch before? "The forest? I...I haven't done anything. I'm not here to harm your forest."

"You are a denizen of my woods," the spirit replied. "You are mine."

"What do you mean?" She skimmed the trees, but it was impossible to pinpoint the source of the voice; it came from all around her.

"I protect what is mine, mortal. You have naught to fear from me."

She caught a fleeting glimpse of shadowy antlers between two trees. She tensed, waiting for the inevitable attack. When it didn't come, she found herself only more anxious.

"You...won't hurt me?" How many times, how many ways, had she asked that of Tyler? How many times had he sworn he'd never hit her again?

How many times had he broken those promises?

The darkness seemed to solidify before her, so complete and thick that it almost hurt her eyes to stare at it. A figure emerged from the ground, and for a moment it towered over her, its massive antlers stretching to either side. Then it sank lower, and a pair of faintly glowing, silver eyes met her gaze.

"So long as you are upon my lands, you have my protection, mortal," the spirit said. "I offer it to you as my oath...but I require something of you first."

Though the spirit's stare was unsettling, it was also strangely familiar. She swallowed thickly. "What…what do you require?"

"*Sophie,*" it purred. "The name of your heart, but not of your birth. Give me your *true* name, mortal."

"How do you know my name?" she asked, taking a step back. "And why should I trust you? You could be lying about all this."

"I have watched since your arrival. Watched and listened." Something moved past her; she felt it, even though she couldn't see it. "And is not the fact that you are still breathing grounds enough for trust, mortal? I destroyed one of the forest's creatures to safeguard you."

Sophie inhaled sharply. She wasn't going crazy—there *had* been something watching her, following her, *touching* her. "I'm sorry," she said quickly. "I didn't mean to…didn't want for it to…"

"Your name," the spirit insisted, "and all is forgiven."

"Josephine. Josephine Davis."

"*Josephine Davis.*" Her name echoed between the trees, but the echo was the rasp of dead leaves, the creaking of ancient boughs. "You have my oath, Josephine Davis. So long as you are within my forest, I will allow no harm to befall you."

Sophie staggered backward as her chest suddenly constricted. Heat flared within her, coalescing around her heart, where it seemed to harden like a shield. She flattened her palm against her chest and stared up at the dark entity. "What was that? What did you just do to me?"

"I have given you my oath, Josephine Davis. It is now yours to carry." A cold hand settled on her shoulder, raising goosebumps beneath her clothing; the sensation wasn't unpleasant.

The memory of shadows writhing over her naked body flickered through Sophie's mind. Her cheeks warmed as she shoved the fragmented dream aside.

She looked up into the spirit's eyes, which were like two dying stars lost in the void of space. "What do I call you?"

47

The spirit was silent for a time, leaving only the forest's night sounds. The air was thick and charged with a strange, thrilling energy.

"Cruce," it finally replied. She felt the word—the name—wash over her, felt the inexplicable, undeniable power tied to it, and shuddered again. Somehow, she knew that he hadn't deceived her. *Cruce* was his *true* name.

She harbored no doubt that this spirit was male.

"So, you've been the one…watching me?"

"Yes."

Stated without apology. Heat spread through Sophie as she recalled all the times she'd felt a presence over the last few days, all the times she'd felt as though she were being watched. It had been Cruce all along. She'd hoped it was a guardian angel looking out for her.

This was beyond anything she might've imagined.

Why am I not more freaked out by this? This is crazy.

Shock. I'm definitely in shock.

Sophie tore her gaze away, looking over the dark tree trunks all around her before returning her attention to the shadow. "I'm lost. Can you show me the way back to my house?"

Cruce's form shifted, becoming bestial; Sophie panicked, seeing the black bear in his shape, but his body lengthened into something vaguely lupine an instant later.

"Come, mortal," he said. When he moved forward, her mind recoiled. Though his shadowy limbs move the way a wolf's would, he *flowed* over the ground like smoke on the wind.

Everything seemed surreal and dreamlike as she followed the spirit through the woods. Cruce was often distinguished from the surrounding shadows only because he was darker. The trees around her felt impossibly tall, and the violet sky overhead cast a faint glow on the trunks that made them seem more phantomlike.

"Are there others like you?" Sophie asked, turning her attention back to the moving shadow. To *Cruce*.

"In other forests, perhaps. I am the sole guardian here."

"Have you ever…left the forest?"

"I am bound to it. I cannot leave its borders."

That explained why she hadn't experienced that *being-watched* sensation in town. "How long have you been here?"

"As long as this forest has been here." His shape had changed again—now he seemed more like a stag, tall and majestic but no less a thing of shadows. "Tens of thousands of autumns, perhaps longer."

"That's a long time."

She crossed her arms over her chest and tucked her hands beneath them. She shivered, but it was due to cold now rather than fear. Her rapidly growing ease with Cruce was beyond her understanding; he was a creature of darkness, an entity that wasn't supposed to be real. She'd seen him kill a bear simply by draping over it, he could make himself invisible, and his shape was constantly changing. Each of those things served as a solid foundation for terror. And yet…she found an inexplicable comfort in his presence. Like a black hole, he drew her in, threatening to swallow her whole, and his deep, guttural voice seemed only to beckon her closer.

"Do you protect everyone living here?" she asked as she climbed over a fallen log.

"I have given my oath only to you, Josephine Davis."

The sensual way his voice caressed her name sent a rush of heat through her. Her breath quickened. "Why only me?"

He reared back, taking on that humanoid shape again, and swept closer to her. His shadows spread wide, like he'd thrown open a cloak or stretched inky wings, before closing around her. Sophie's breath caught in her throat; she would learn firsthand the agony the bear had endured in its final moments.

"Because you are *mine*," Cruce said, his voice merging with the darkness surrounding her.

Sophie squeezed her eyes shut, her body paralyzed by fear and thrumming with anticipation. He was cold, so cold, but his touch was light and gentle, and his voice rumbled straight to her center…

How could she be so deeply frightened and aroused at the same time?

A cool tendril caressed her cheek. "We are here, Sophie."

She opened her eyes to find herself released from his shadowy embrace. Her cabin was just ahead, the light from the front windows illuminating two long strips of the dirt driveway.

Had they really traveled so far, or had she not been as deep in the woods as she'd thought?

"Thank you," she said, but he was gone when she turned to face him. Sophie shifted her gaze to the tree line, searching for a patch of shadows with two silver, orb-like eyes, but the light from the window disrupted her night vision just enough to make it impossible to distinguish any subtle differences in the blackness.

Rubbing her arms, she walked across the driveway and up the steps onto the porch. Once inside the cabin, she locked the door behind her and leaned against it. The sensation of his touch hadn't faded. It was imprinted upon her body, just as his name was emblazoned upon her soul.

His words played over and over in her mind.

Because you are mine.

Sophie tilted her head back and closed her eyes.

No. No, I can't. I can't let anyone control me again.

She'd barely made it out alive last time. This time, she feared the damage could end up being far greater.

· · ·

CRUCE LINGERED at the edge of the woods and watched as Sophie moved about inside the cabin. Her actions made little difference to him; he was transfixed by *her* and simultaneously stupefied by his own decisions.

Why had he so easily given over his true name? In his world, the world of spirts, fae, and magic, names were things of great power. That power carried into the mortal realm, though its potency was diminished there. He'd handed her the potential to control and manipulate him, to bend him to her will. Her true name enabled Cruce to *influence* her slightly more, had allowed him to give her a real, binding oath, but mortals were not bound by the same rules as beings such as himself. In his curse-stricken form, he lacked the magic to do her any real harm through use of her name.

Sophie walked across the main room of the cabin as though in a daze. Cruce watched as she filled a kettle with water and placed it atop the stove. She leaned forward with her hands on the counter and eyes unfocused for many moments before finally shaking herself and igniting the burner.

Cruce told himself it had been a calculated move on his part; he'd offered his name to put her at ease and gain some of her trust. Sophie was a modern mortal; her kind no longer held to the old ways. She was ignorant of the laws that bound him and didn't know how to weaponize his true name.

Humanity had forgotten the ancient rituals and traditions, and that was to the benefit of beings like Cruce.

She returned to the sink and filled a glass with water, sipping it as she stared out the window.

Those justifications didn't hold true when he reflected upon them further. Somehow, what Cruce had done, the immense risk he'd taken, felt *right*. His true name had been a precious, closely guarded thing, a secret for eons. He'd revealed it only to the fae queen, who'd later used it to curse him. He did not fear the same from Josephine Davis. Though he knew little about her, and she knew *nothing* about him, she was the best person to hold his true name.

Small animals skittered through the surrounding forest, each of them familiar to their fallen lord. He also knew every plant and tree; the sounds of their leaves and branches made music wholly unique to his forest and this season. Normally, he'd give himself over to the woods, lose himself within them, and attempt to forget his curse for a little while.

But tonight, thoughts of Sophie consumed Cruce. The warmth he'd felt through her clothes lingered within him, defiant of the cold, and her delicious scent remained on the crisp night air. He longed to learn the feel of her entire body one tiny piece at a time. Despite his lack of a physical form, she made him feel as though his blood were heated, and his desire for her only increased each time he drew near to her.

He moved silently through the undergrowth to position himself near the side window as she walked out of the kitchen and sat on the sofa, a steaming mug in her hands. He wouldn't go to her yet, not while the lights were on, but once she retired to her chamber to sleep…

All Hallows Eve would come in seven days. Cruce didn't plan to waste any of the time between now and then.

CHAPTER FOUR

SHADOWY HANDS and tendrils smoothed over Sophie's body. She was awash with pleasure, reduced to a writhing creature incapable of thought as a tidal wave of sensation carried her away. She moaned, sighed, and begged, craving more, needing more.

The shadows brushed over her breasts, stroking and sucking her nipples. Jolts of pleasure flashed through her, heat coalesced in her core, and her sex pulsed. She teetered on the brink of oblivion with no release in sight.

Twin wisps of shadow grasped her knees and parted them. Another tendril trailed down her stomach and over her pelvis to delve into the folds of her sex and tease her clit. Sophie gasped, eyes flying open, and he was there, standing before her.

Cruce.

Huge, black antlers grew from his head as he shifted closer to her, wedging his hips between her legs to force them wide. His shadowy hands, tipped with pointed claws, settled on her thighs and slowly ran upwards. He brushed his thumbs over the sensitive flesh of her sex before capturing her wrists and holding them captive to either side of her head.

He leaned over Sophie; he was a mass of restless, hungry shadows,

consuming everything in his path—the light, the air, Sophie herself.
Cruce became her entire world. Something pressed against the
entrance of her sex, something thick and hard.

"You are mine, Josephine." His deep voice resonated through Sophie
before he thrust his hips forward and slammed his cock into her.

Sophie woke with a gasp, her body tense and shuddering in
the throes of an orgasm. Waves of pleasure swept through her.
She filled the room with her cries, which escalated in volume
until she finally tumbled off her peak and could produce no
sounds but those of her desperate, panting breaths.

She lay there, stunned, feeling the wetness on her thighs.
She'd never come so hard in her life. How had a *dream* brought
her to that point?

That's all it was, right? A dream? That's all everything was...

The walk in the woods, the bear attack, meeting Cruce,
and...the sex, it had all been a dream. Even though she recalled
it in vivid detail, even though she could still feel the caress of
shadows on her flesh, even though she could still feel him *inside*
her, it couldn't have been anything but a wild dream.

Her sex throbbed, aching with unfulfilled need despite her
toe-curling climax. She slid a hand down her stomach. She paused
as her fingers dipped under the waistband of her underwear.

The temptation was there, the desire, but she knew that an
orgasm at her own fingers wouldn't give her the satisfaction for
which she yearned.

It'd feel hollow.

Removing her hand, Sophie sat up and slipped off the bed.
Once again, she'd soaked her sheets. With a groan, she removed
the bedding, dumped it—along with her bottoms—into the
washer, and got it started.

"Two nights in a row," she muttered, shaking her head. "This
better not become a habit."

Despite her lingering need for true satisfaction, she felt

surprisingly refreshed. Having to run a load of laundry every day was a major downside, but there seemed to be some perks to waking up like this.

After cleaning up and dressing, Sophie entered the kitchen. She opened the cabinet to grab her favorite mug only to find its spot empty. Frowning, she glanced at the sink. The mug was sitting within, and the kettle was still atop the stove with a box of teabags on the counter nearby.

"Just a dream," she said softly as she put the tea away and emptied the kettle.

Maybe I was sleepwalking?

She hadn't sleepwalked in ages, not since she was a kid. When her somnambulance had been at its worst, her parents had installed a lock high up on the front and back doors to keep her from slipping outside in the middle of the night. She'd grown out of the habit years ago, but maybe it was coming back? It wouldn't surprise her considering the amount of stress and trauma she'd experienced over the last few years.

Sighing, she turned to look over the living room. Her gaze paused when it fell on the scarf and knitted sweater she'd worn the night before. They were draped over the back of the sofa with broken bits of brown leaves clinging to them. Her sneakers were on the floor just below; she normally kept them near the front door.

Sophie slowly turned back to the counter and went through her morning ritual of making coffee and breakfast like an automaton. Either parts of last night hadn't been a dream and she'd just been too tired to keep it all straight, or she'd been sleepwalking. She hoped it was the former; the latter was too frightening. Who knew what dangers lurked outside in the...*shadows*...

The aroma of brewing coffee helped her shake off those thoughts. She inhaled deeply, letting the smell ease her nerves.

Taking a new mug down from the cupboard, she poured her coffee and mixed in some of her favorite creamer.

She stepped into her slippers, tossed the throw blanket over her shoulders, and took the mug outside. Walking off the porch, she basked in the morning sunlight with the mug nestled between her hands to ward off the chill. She scanned the surrounding trees. Nothing moved but the occasional falling leaf. None of the shadows were as dark or as consuming as they'd been in her dreams.

"Hello?" she called. Just hearing her voice echo through the crisp air made her feel silly. "I was dreaming. There's no such thing as forest spirits."

Her mind had been playing tricks on her; the years of abuse, the horrific night during which she'd almost died, and the uncertainty of trying to get away before Tyler was out of jail were finally crashing down upon her now that she had time to stop and think. It wasn't pleasant, but it was part of the healing process.

Besides, everything was so pretty and luminous in the daylight. She'd just let the nighttime gloom pair with her paranoia to get out of hand.

"It was just a dream."

"So, how are you feeling today?" Kate asked. She was looking down at her hand as she painted her nails, attempting to seem nonchalant, but Sophie didn't miss the hint of worry in her voice.

"Great! I got a ton of words in today, and I think might even finish the first draft by the end of next week. It feels so good to be writing again." Sophie stood up from the sofa and carried the laptop into the kitchen. She set it on the counter and adjusted the screen. "Why do you ask?"

Kate glanced at her. "Well, I got a call last night from a woman scared out of her wits."

Sophie blushed. "I know. I was hoping that was part of the dream, too."

"Hey. You know I'm here for you no matter what. Don't *ever* hesitate to call me, even if you think it's nothing." Kate closed the nail polish and leaned closer to the camera. "Soph, have you considered talking to someone?"

"I'm talking to you," Sophie said with exaggerated innocence and a smile.

"You *know* what I mean. Someone more qualified to help you with your problems. If you're suddenly sleepwalking again, or... questioning what's real and what's not—"

"I'm not crazy, Kate."

Am I?

Kate's eyes widened. "No, of course you're not! I'd never think that of you. You've just been through a lot, Sophie. A professional might be able to help you work through everything you've endured. Help you work through your trauma."

Sophie clutched the edge of the counter hard enough to make her fingers ache. "I talk to you, Kate."

"I know," Kate said gently, "but not about everything."

"You don't need to hear *everything*. You've seen enough, and you've taken so much of it onto yourself already." Sophie's eyes stung; she resisted the urge to rub them. "This is all going to work out for the best, and I'll never have to worry about him again."

And I have the forest spirit's protection.

But that wasn't *real!* She couldn't depend upon an...an *imaginary friend.*

"Is he still there?" Sophie asked.

"Yeah. He hasn't left the house today as far as I know. He's had a few people over, but no one I recognize."

Much of Sophie's tension eased. So long as Tyler stayed there, she was safe here. "Any plans for Halloween this year?"

Kate's frown sent a clear message—*I don't like you changing the subject*—but it gave way to a cheeky grin. "I have a date."

"Really?" Sophie smiled with vicarious excitement. Kate had had a few casual flings since she and Sophie became friends, but she only *dated* when she was serious about a guy.

"Yep. There's a company party on Halloween night, and *this* girl's got a plus one."

Sophie chuckled. "What are you going as this year? A sexy nun? Sexy nurse? Harem girl?"

Kate laughed. "Close! Hold on a minute." She disappeared, giving Sophie a view of Kate's office wall.

There was a bookcase on each side of the window behind Kate's desk. One was filled with books and files pertaining to Kate's work as an accountant, and the other, to Sophie's constant delight, was filled to the brim with romance novels— including all the books Sophie had written. As soon as Kate had discovered Sophie was an author, she'd purchased and read every single one. It had been Kate who pushed her to begin writing again after everything with Tyler.

The camera spun around, and Kate stepped back so she was fully in frame and posed with her hands on her hips and her feet wide. Sophie's jaw dropped. Kate's long, dark hair was swept back and held in place by a golden headband with a red star at its center. She wore a shiny red, sleeveless corset that pushed up her breasts, a wide golden belt, and the tiniest, *shiniest* blue booty shorts Sophie had ever seen. She would have killed for legs like Kate's.

"What do you think?" Kate asked, turning around to give Sophie a three-sixty. "Do I look like a sexy superhero?"

"Wow. You look amazing!"

"Really?" She grinned, turning the computer back toward the bookcases as she took her seat.

Sophie wiggled her brows. "I'd do you."

They both laughed.

"So, who is this guy?" Sophie asked.

"Actually..." Kate cleared her throat and dropped her gaze. "He was your nurse while you were in the hospital."

Sophie's eyes widened. "No way! Steve?"

Kate's cheeks flushed, and she nodded. "Yep. Steve."

Steve had always had a smile for Sophie. He'd been so sweet, kind, and considerate while Sophie had recovered from the damage Tyler had done. He was a single dad with two kids; during their many conversations, he'd revealed that his wife had cheated on him three years before, and they'd gone through a rough divorce. He hadn't been interested in dating afterward, putting all his focus into his two girls...until he met Kate.

He'd tried to hide his interest in Kate when she came to visit, but his normally smooth, easy-going demeanor had turned into a stammering, awkward mess on more than one occasion. Sophie had found it endearing.

"It's been months since I left the hospital," Sophie said.

"We exchanged numbers while you were still in there, and we've been taking things slow since then. Texting and talking and...Facetiming." Kate's smile told Sophie all she needed to know; this was *serious*. "We haven't gone out in person yet, but..."

"I'm so happy for you!"

They spoke for another half hour as Sophie made dinner, laughing throughout, and Sophie felt a hundred times lighter by the time they said their goodbyes. She finished eating and cleaned up. After checking all the locks, she went to take a shower.

She let the water run to warm it up as she undressed and tossed her dirty clothes in the hamper. As she was about to step into the tub, she caught a glimpse of herself in the mirror. She frowned at the mottled, purple bruise on her side. She pressed her hand over it; the spot was slightly larger than her hand, and though it was tender, the pain wasn't unbearable. Where had it come from? Why hadn't she noticed it before?

The bear.

No. That didn't happen.

If it'd been a bear, she'd be dead. There was no way she would've survived a bear attack with nothing but a bruise.

Cruce.

No! He wasn't real. There were no spirit-men made of living shadow lurking in the woods. It was a fantasy, a delusion.

So why did she feel like someone was watching her even now? Wasn't that a delusion, too?

"It's just my imagination adjusting to the new place, nothing more. I'm not going crazy." She stared at the bruise. "I fell and hit my side on the floor while I was sleepwalking, and my subconscious turned it into a bear attack in my dream. That's all."

Why did that explanation feel *less* rational than the shadow-man bear attack?

Because it's the same sort of story I told people who noticed the bruises Tyler left on me.

Looking away in disgust, she shoved those thoughts aside and stepped into the shower.

The hot water felt wonderful, instantly soothing her. She sighed and turned the heat up a little more before cleaning herself.

As she rinsed away the soap, Sophie's thoughts strayed back to her dream. She recalled the feel of shadowy tendrils gliding along her limbs, the thrilling tingle of their chilly touch, and Cruce looming over her like a dark, lust-inducing god.

Before Sophie knew it, her hands were massaging her breasts. She'd resisted the urge this morning, but she couldn't help touching herself now. Her nipples were responsive, her skin overly sensitive beneath the hot water, and her sex clenched with need.

Closing her eyes, she tilted her head back. Water ran in rivulets down her chest and back.

Sophie cupped her breasts, caressing them, and tweaked her nipples, imagining it was Cruce's hands upon her. A low, needy moan escaped her. A strange but pleasurable sensation trailed down her torso, icy and hot at once, setting her skin ablaze. She didn't think; she just *felt*.

She tilted her head to the side, allowing more water to flow over her shoulder and down toward her pelvis, and parted her thighs. The sensation intensified, dipping to brush along her folds, the pressure concentrating on her clit before slipping *inside* her. Sophie squeezed her breasts and gasped as pleasure threatened to overcome her.

She opened her eyes abruptly.

It was dark.

Her body tensed, her hands stilled, and she inhaled sharply. The stream of water continued unbroken, but there was something *else* caressing her.

Faint light stole into the bathroom through the window, and as her eyes adjusted to it, she looked down. Deep, dark shadows obscured the tub, surrounding her body like mist. They sculpted to her every curve, their cool touch counteracted by the hot water passing through them to shower her skin.

This was what had been touching her.

Sophie jerked back and screamed, slapping at the shadow. Her hands connected with nothing solid until her palm struck her own thigh.

"Be at ease, mortal," said the voice from last night—Cruce's voice. Its deep bass was amplified by the walls of the shower, vibrating through her to heighten her pleasure despite her startlement.

She turned around. "Oh my God!"

He stood tall, as imposing as he was alluring, a black abyss exuding sensuality and calling her into his dark embrace. It seemed impossible that he could fit in the bathroom; he was too large, too powerful, too otherworldly. The faint points of light that must've been his eyes stared down at her from within the darkness.

Cruce chuckled, and she felt his touch just beneath her ear, trailing lazily down her neck. "I can be your god," he purred, "and lavish you with pleasures beyond your wildest dreams."

Sophie panted as her climax built, threatening to burst through her. She squeezed her thighs together and swatted at the tendrils of shadow stroking her sex. "Stop it," she rasped.

To her shock, his motions paused. Sophie's hips nearly bucked of their own accord; her body needed *more*. Her annoyance at her reaction solidified her resolve.

"Is this not what you desire, Josephine Davis?"

"I didn't ask for this." Her words trembled faintly; she shook with unfulfilled desire, with the need for release.

"Asking and wanting are not one in the same." The shadowy hold on her tightened subtly. He leaned closer, his eyes boring into hers. "I *feel* your desire, your need. You need not ask for pleasure. I offer it to you freely."

"I won't be manipulated by you." She clenched her jaw, forcing her body to still its treacherous movements, and met his gaze. "I want you out, Cruce."

"Out?" he rasped. "Josephine…"

"Get out of my home."

He released an inhuman growl, and his shadows receded rapidly. His form seemed to diminish as he withdrew from the shower. The curtain moved as though in a breeze, and the faint night glow from outside brightened slightly, but the overhead light did not come back on.

Sophie swallowed. The rapid pounding of her heart was underscored by the sound of water falling to the floor of the tub, but otherwise, all was silent.

Cruce was gone.

I'm hallucinating. That's all this is. The lightbulb just burned out, or—

Something roared outside; it was a layered sound, and it chilled Sophie to the bone. She didn't know of any animals that could make a call like *that*.

She hurried out of the tub and nearly slipped on her way to the light switch. The bulbs over the mirror flared on. Momentarily blinded, she extended her arms and returned to the shower to turn off the water. Then she wrapped a towel around herself and retreated to the corner, where she slid down into a sitting position and hugged her legs close to her chest.

It was real. *He* was real. She wasn't crazy or overly imaginative. There was something out there, something that had been watching her from the moment she'd arrived.

Another roar sounded outside, followed by a guttural snarl.

She'd angered him. Would he recant his oath? Why hadn't he done so already? Why wasn't he in here now, tearing her to shreds, or doing whatever it was he'd done to the bear?

Why had he left when he clearly hadn't wanted to?

That confused her the most.

When she was sure he wasn't going to come charging back into the cabin, she slowly pulled herself to her feet. Clutching the edges of the towel to her chest, Sophie moved to the door and opened it. She peered outside and into the living room and kitchen. Only a single light was on—her small desk lamp. She scrutinized every shadow from her place in the doorway; there was no sign of him.

Racing out of the bathroom, she turned on every light in the house and closed every curtain. Once that was done, she retreated into her bedroom, heart pounding. She held her breath, listening for sounds from outside, but heard nothing.

Was he gone?

She dried off and dressed quickly before retrieving her baseball bat from the corner. Lifting the bat, she stared down at it for several moments. Her lips fell into a deep frown.

What the hell am I going to do with this? He's made of shadow!

Sophie returned the bat to its place, climbed onto the bed, and pulled the covers over her head. This was what kids did when they were frightened, right? You were safe while hiding under the blanket, untouchable, invisible.

She had no means by which to mark the passage of time as she waited.

Nothing happened.

Did he tell me the truth? Does he really mean me no harm?

To make matters worse, her body still throbbed with lust, her sex aching with unfulfilled desire.

CHAPTER FIVE

FURY ROILED WITHIN CRUCE, disrupting and distorting his form as he stalked the woods around the cabin. His anger was fueled by his own unsated appetite—he wanted more of Sophie, to *touch* her, to relish her warmth. He wanted her scent, which had been sweetened by the perfume of her arousal, to sweep through him. She'd yearned for what he'd attempted to give her; he'd *felt* it.

And she'd rejected him anyway.

His being thrummed with new energy—with energy from Sophie. But he hadn't drained her, hadn't taken. Somehow, their intimacy, her arousal, had poured fresh strength into him, as potent as any he'd taken from other humans but more satisfying because of its source.

Now, it only heightened his rage.

He moved around the rear of the cabin. She'd drawn all the curtains, but the lights were still on inside. She was awake; he wasn't sure how he knew, but he was certain of it.

No one had *ever* exercised such dominance over him—not even the queen when she'd cursed him. It stung to have been turned away so thoroughly by a mortal.

69

That his want for the same mortal hadn't diminished was infuriating.

Whether wittingly or not, she'd invoked the ancient laws to which he remained bound. Though her home stood within the borders of his forest, it belonged to Sophie, and she was master within its walls. Just as the queen had been master within her own court despite it laying inside Cruce's domain.

The reminder of the queen, of his curse, stoked the fires of his fury. He longed for an outlet for his anger, but there could be none. Any damage he inflicted upon his forest and its creatures was a direct blow to himself. His power, though sealed by the curse, remained connected to the health and balance of his forest. Each time he drained one of its plants or beasts, he gained a temporary rush of energy, and his domain weakened just a little more because the natural order had been disrupted by his feeding.

He prowled the area around the cabin restlessly, his attention fixated on the windows, watching for any movement within and waiting with unreasonable anticipation for even the briefest glimpse of Sophie. In time, the sky lightened with approaching dawn.

Cruce ignored the feeling of diminishment that swept over him as the sun rose, continuing his agitated patrol. Not long after sunrise, he spied movement through the tiny gap in one of the front window curtains. Sophie emerged from her bed chamber, but she didn't step onto the porch with her hot beverage to enjoy the morning light as she had each day since her arrival. She didn't look outside, didn't so much as touch the curtains.

He darted between the ever-shifting patches of shadow beneath the canopy while the day slowly passed, longing for her to come outside, longing to go to her, clinging to his rage throughout.

Just the thought of entering her home again sent a strange, foreboding ripple through him; her willpower in casting him out was as strong as any warding spell he'd ever encountered. Trying to break it would bring only pain.

She spent most of the day at her desk, staring at the strange device through which she'd conversed with her friend, Kate. He wasn't sure what she was doing with it—she manipulated its controls with speed and familiarity, but his view was so limited by the curtains that he could not see the screen from any angle.

Cruce's fury smoldered; she was willfully ignoring his presence, was ignoring her own desires simply to spite him. He was Lord of the Forest, ancient and powerful, awe-inspiring and terrifying, protector and destroyer within his realm. Who was she to pretend he did not exist? Who was she to spurn *him*?

And yet he was powerless. Whatever Cruce had been, he was merely a shade now, a cursed thing, and this mortal had overcome him.

The clear, cerulean sky allowed pure sunlight to stream down over the forest, sapping the strength Cruce had received from Sophie as the day wore on. His movements slowed, as they always did when it was so bright. He did not release his anger, and he refused to find a more comfortable location where he could take shelter and await the relief evening would bring.

She had to come outside eventually. When she did, he would be waiting, and he'd...

What would he do? What *could* he do? He was oathbound to protect Sophie, and despite his anger, the thought of doing her harm remained sickening to him. What sort of position had he placed himself in?

He cast his doubts aside; they would do him no good. He wasn't meant to suffer doubt or indecision. He wasn't meant to answer to the whims of mortals...

SOMETIME AFTER THE sun had set and darkness had descended upon the forest, Sophie opened her front door. Cruce watched from the shadows as light spilled through the closed screen door to fall upon a wide swath of the hard-packed dirt and damp, fallen leaves in front of her home. She stood in the doorframe, silhouetted by the golden glow from within, looking confident and powerful. For that instant, she seemed a queen in her own right.

How would she look with a crown of autumn leaves atop her auburn hair, striding through the trees, head held high and eyes bright? How would it feel to have her walking beside him, arms intertwined?

"I know you're there," she said, eyes shifting as though searching the darkness.

Somehow, he held himself back. *She* was not in control. He would not play this game, would not allow her to ignore him all day and then hurry to her side when she finally deigned to acknowledge him.

"Come out. We need to talk." She folded her lips inward and bit them. Her expression warred with itself, producing a line between her brows. "Come to me now, Cruce."

Her voice caressed his name, but no matter how sweet she made it sound, the command was clear. Bristling, he surged across the open ground and drew himself up in front of her door. She flinched back as he leaned toward her, hunching his tall figure to meet her gaze.

"What have you to say, mortal?" he snarled.

"It's true," she breathed, eyes wide.

"*What* is true?"

"That using your true name would compel you."

Cruce growled. "You toy with dangerous forces if you mean to control me, human."

"No, I—" She snapped her mouth shut, glanced away from him, then straightened her posture. "We need to set boundaries."

He dipped his eyes toward the threshold; he was powerless to cross it. He lifted his gaze back to her.

"What you did wasn't right. This is my home, my...my body." She swallowed. "You had no right to touch me like that."

"It was what you desired. You craved my touch, Josephine Davis. You crave it still."

"No, I don't!"

Cruce could taste her lie.

"Whether or not I did," she continued, "I *never* asked for it, never invited it. You came into my home and a-assaulted me. I came here to get away from—" She pressed her lips together and looked away from him, but Cruce caught the shimmer of tears in her eyes. "I came here to be safe. Yesterday, I didn't feel safe."

The sight of her tears struck him deep; a strange, constricting feeling spread through his being. "I am oathbound to protect you."

"But what will protect me from you?"

"I have done you no harm. Just as I vowed."

"Those are just *words*, and I'm sure you have your own... supernatural definitions you've put into place in your head to twist them to your advantage. There are a lot of ways to hurt someone. Not all of them are physical."

He wanted this to be nothing more than her bending the truth, nothing more than her attempt at manipulation to gain more from him. He *wanted* her to have some ulterior motive. Cruce was used to such maneuvers—they'd been as much a part of his world as magic. Spirits and fae constantly attempted to bend the laws into their favor, to gain advantage over one another based on such subtleties.

But he knew at his core that this was the truth. *Her* truth.

"Come outside, Josephine Davis."

She met his gaze again and pressed a hand against the screen door, pushing it open only a sliver before pausing. "Why?"

73

"So I may prove that I mean you no harm." That was only part of it, though. He wanted to touch her, to feel her heat, to revel in the responses of her body. He had no intentions of draining her, but there were so many ways he wanted to use her for his own amusement.

He longed to do all the things she *claimed* she didn't want.

"And you can't lie because you're...fae, right?" she asked.

"I am not fae," he replied, "I am something other. The Lord of the Forest."

"But you can be controlled by your true name."

"Many beings can be controlled by their true name, if it is wielded by one knowledgeable enough."

"Y-you have mine. Can...can you control me?"

"No." He sank lower, shadows writhing restlessly over the porch, desperate for another feel of her.

"But you would if you were able, wouldn't you?"

"Yes." He eased closer to the screen door, his eyes boring into hers. "I want you, Josephine Davis."

Her pupils dilated, and a soft breath escaped her parted lips. She wanted him, too. Her attempts to display the contrary couldn't hide her true feelings.

"Then why would I join you outside? How can I trust you when you openly admit that you'd use my name against me? When you say that you...you *want* me?"

"Would my desire for you be condemned in your mortal realm?" he asked, brushing tendrils of shadow over the screen. "I am not *Tyler*."

She drew back, eyes gleaming with sudden terror, and the screen door banged shut.

"I have given you my oath, Josephine Davis. So long as you are within my woods, you are under my protection from any threat—mortal or otherwise. He will do you no harm here."

"How do you—"

"As I have admitted, I have watched and listened. I cannot

pretend to understand most of your mortal affairs, but I understand that he has hurt you, and you fear he will do so again."

She was silent for a time, her eyes moving over his form. He felt unclean beneath her gaze, unworthy, and wondered what she saw as she looked at him. This was not his body, this was not Cruce; this was his curse. A curse that had caused him great anger and bitterness, but never shame. Not until that moment.

"If you're not fae, then you can lie, can't you?" she asked. "And why would you protect me when I know your name? I could use it against you."

"I may lie, yes, but I have not lied to you, Josephine Davis. My instinct was to trust you with my name, as I have trusted only one other before." He leaned even closer, and her scent teased him through the screen. "Was I mistaken to place my trust in you?"

"That...depends."

He withdrew from the doorway, studying her posture, her expression. Despite her apparent fear, there was strength at her center—the iron resolve he'd sensed in her life force. "Upon what?"

"The boundaries I set. If you cross them, I will use whatever means necessary to protect myself from you."

She knew how to cast him out of her home, but what else did she know? What else was she capable of? He couldn't tell if she was speaking from knowledge or empty bravado, but he found himself strangely thrilled, either way.

"What *boundaries* do you propose, mortal?"

She held up a hand and tallied her fingers as she spoke. "Do not eavesdrop on my conversations. Do not enter my home uninvited. Do not grope me without invita—um, actually, just *don't* grope me." Her cheeks flushed. "And don't...invade my dreams."

Cruce eased forward. "You have dreamed of me?"

Somehow, her skin reddened further, coming to nearly

match her auburn hair. She looked away and said nothing; it was all the confirmation he needed.

Magic had a multitude of effects on mortals, some unpredictable, but influencing a human's dreams typically required a concentrated effort—the working of a spell. He possessed no such ability under his curse.

He recalled the state in which she'd woken two days before, the first time he'd scented her arousal. Had she been dreaming of him then?

What was it about this mortal that so drew him to her? What was it that seemed to connect them so deeply?

"That was not *my* doing, Josephine. Perhaps it is your heart revealing your true desire."

"If you're not doing it, then you don't know what they were about," she said. "You could be killing me in my dreams for all you know."

He chuckled. "A fitting play on words. Does not your kind sometimes refer to it as the *little death?*"

Sophie stepped back and raised her hands to her cheeks. "Oh my God, how do you even *know* that?"

She'd been attempting to deflect the line of conversation, but Cruce had dealt with masters of such tactics. Sophie had much more to learn if she meant to guard her truth. But he found her inability to mask her inner thoughts endearing. The honesty—even if it was inadvertent some of the time—was a refreshing change from what he'd been used to for most of his existence.

"I must propose a condition of my own before I agree to anything," he said.

She eyed him warily. "What...condition?"

"I have given my name into your holding. It is to be shared with no one else under *any* circumstances. And you will not use it against me unless you feel wholeheartedly that I am in violation of your *boundaries.*"

She nodded. "I swear. I won't share it with anyone else or use it against you unless I feel it is necessary."

"Then I accept your boundaries, Josephine Davis. We must seal the agreement."

"Okay. Do I... Do we need to seal it in blood or something?"

He looked down at the wisps of shadow that comprised him, then back up at her.

She frowned. "Oh. Sorry."

"Open the door, Sophie."

She glanced at the door, hesitation flashing in her eyes. She undoubtedly feared him, but her curiosity was stronger. Flattening a hand on the board running across its center, she pushed, slowly opening the screen door wide.

Cruce moved forward, his shadows flickering and writhing, and brushed a tendril over the heated skin of her arm. She sucked in a sharp breath but did not pull back.

"Lean forward," he said, "over the threshold."

Keeping her eyes locked with his, she did as he'd instructed.

Focusing all his willpower into the endeavor, he forced his shadows into a form as close to his physical body as he could, drawing in the wisps to solidify himself. Were the full moon not so near, he would have been unable to accomplish it with such relative ease.

Dipping his head, he brushed his lips over hers. Her warmth arced across his face, spreading throughout his illusory body, crackling with electric energy. He felt her pleasure, her uncertainty, her fear, but most of all, her desire. It flowed into him, blasting him with new strength and shoving aside his ever-present hunger.

Her eyes widened, and her lips parted. He took advantage of what she unwittingly offered by sliding his tongue into her mouth, exploring for a moment before the sensation, the power, was too much, and he lost his tenuous hold on his form.

He withdrew from her as his shadows roiled, unable to settle upon a shape.

Sophie stepped back, covering her mouth with a hand and staring at him with dazed eyes. The screen door swung shut with an even louder bang. "You kissed me."

Cruce hummed deeply. Sophie's taste and scent lingered within him, and her life essence pulsed stronger than ever. He did not understand how he'd taken from her without doing her harm. "Our pact is made, Josephine Davis."

When she did not reply, he moved a bit closer. "Will you invite me inside?"

Her eyes widened further, and his words seemed to snap her out of her daze. "No! N-not tonight."

"We've much more to dis—"

She slammed the interior door, plunging his section of porch into relative darkness. Her life force radiated from the other side of the door, and he pictured her standing with her back against it, her heart racing.

Cruce laughed as he slowly retreated to the trees. His mortal was intriguing, beguiling, and entertaining. Never had he been inclined to give so much while receiving so little in return.

But that wasn't true, was it? He was conceding to her demands, yes, but he'd gain her company in return. Less than a week ago, he wouldn't have thought time with a mortal could be worthwhile. Now, he possessed a very different opinion.

He had five days until the full moon on All Hallows Eve. Five days to convince her to eliminate these boundaries. Five days to convince her that she belonged to *him*.

CHAPTER SIX

INDECISION CHURNED within Sophie as she stared at the door. The bright morning sunlight streamed in from the east side of the house, filling it with a golden glow. Outside, the shadows were long, but they were not deep. There was nothing to worry about. This was not Cruce's time.

Right?

She tentatively reached for the doorknob only to pull her hand back for the third time. A frustrated growl tore from her throat. Cruce was real, without a doubt, and he'd sworn to protect her. But she still feared him. Things like him weren't supposed to exist.

"Why am I being such a *coward*?"

Because I just found out that the supernatural is very *real, and* very *interested in me.*

The answer should've been that easy, but she knew truth in her heart.

Tyler.

Her soon-to-be ex-husband had instilled her with a fear of men, and her recognition of that fear's irrationality made no difference. Even separated by a few hundred miles, he was still *taking* from her.

When would it end? When would she say *enough is enough*?

Cruce wasn't human, but he was undoubtedly masculine. Confident, possessive, and domineering. Everything she'd been taught to submit to. Everything she'd learned to fear.

And yet, he'd given her his name. *She* had the power, not him. He couldn't control her with magic—or at least he *said* he couldn't—and she wouldn't allow herself to be manipulated. She'd not relent to his demands. If anything happened between them, it would be on Sophie's terms.

So why did she feel so drawn to him? Cruce's magnetism was something out of a romance book, the sort of thing she'd built a career writing about. The sort of thing that wasn't supposed to happen in the real world.

He'd been the subject of her last thought before she fell asleep, and his name had been on her lips when she awoke to another climax. She'd dreamed of him more intensely than ever last night. Sophie's mouth still tingled with the memory of his cold kiss.

Taking in a deep breath, Sophie steeled herself, pulled open the front door, and stepped out onto her porch. As she walked down the steps and onto the dirt driveway, the warm sunlight touched her skin, an immediate contrast to the cool, crisp air. Her gaze skimmed the tree line, but she doubted she'd ever spot Cruce unless he wanted to be seen.

"Are you there?" she asked, folding her arms over her chest. She hadn't brought her throw, hadn't even considered it. Her entire routine had been disrupted; Cruce had largely dominated her thoughts since she woke.

"Yes." His voice was the wind sighing through the leaves, flowing over her in a gentle caress. "I am here."

She jumped when she heard him; though she'd called to him, and his voice had been soft, part of her still wanted to believe this wasn't real. Hearing him talk made it far more difficult to pretend he didn't exist. She turned toward the sound of his voice and swept her gaze from side to side. After several moments, she noticed a slight distortion in the air, more like the blur of heat baking off the hood of a car in the summer than the deep, writhing shadows she'd seen of him thus far.

"Why are you so...different?" she asked.

"The sunlight," he replied. Even his voice was *less.*

"Does it weaken you?"

"It is an aspect of my curse."

Sophie frowned. "Your curse? What kind of curse?"

His faint form moved past her, and part of him brushed across her calf, producing an echo of the chill his touch normally left in its wake. "The kind bestowed by displeased queens upon those who cross them."

She turned to follow his movements. It wouldn't be hard to lose him in this light. "Queens? Like...ladies of the forest?" She refused to acknowledge the flare of jealousy in her gut. It didn't make sense! He was a shadow, a creature, something inhuman. He wasn't anything to her...

"No. It was the queen of a fae court." He moved into the porch's shade, and his form grew immediately more defined.

"So, you weren't always like"—she waved a hand toward him —"*this?*"

Cruce pressed against the wall and drew his shadows together. "No, I was not always like this. I had a physical form and could cross between the mortal realm and the spirit realm as I wished."

"What did you do? Why were you cursed?"

He was silent for several moments, his restless shadows expanding and contracting, darkening and fading. "I entered a pact with a fae queen. She required a secure location to establish her court, well away from mortal eyes. I desired her powerful glamours to obfuscate my forest from the humans who sought to encroach upon it. Together, it seemed, we could prosper."

Sophie stepped closer to the porch but kept well within the sunlight. "What happened?"

"Time passed. The seasons changed. And your kind grew ever bolder in their advances. They felled my trees, hunted my animals, and seemed increasingly unconcerned with the queen's glamour. My power diminished. Hers remained. I felt as though I was not receiving my end of the bargain. I blamed her, oblivious as I was to the tenacity of mortals. So, I sought to reclaim what I had gifted her. Her court was within my realm, so it should have been *mine.*" His shadows bristled at that last word, jutting out like spikes before receding.

"I mistakenly thought myself strong enough to overthrow her. To claim her court, and thereby her crown and the power it commanded. Then I would've been able to protect what belonged to me." He sank low, spreading over the floorboards. "But in her court, she was queen. And I had broken my oath, which had been made upon our true names. She cursed me for my betrayal. Made me into what you see now."

Sophie studied him warily. "After all that, why would you give me your name?"

"As I said, my instincts are to trust you."

"Did you...feel the same about the queen?"

His shadows drifted closer to her. "It was not a matter of trust. It was a matter of necessity. We required one another for survival, and...she enjoyed my company in her bedchamber."

"Oh."

I don't care. Nope. Not at all. Why would I?

Don't. Care. At. All.

So why did it feel like a punch to the gut?

Sophie clenched her hands.

He produced a low, thoughtful hum. "Is my mortal jealous?"

"No," she said quickly. Too quickly. "And I'm not *your* mortal."

"Your denial does not alter the truth, Josephine Davis."

"Why do you keep saying my name like that?"

"Because it is your true name."

She arched her brow. "Would you like me to speak your name out loud at every turn, then?"

"So long as we are alone, you may speak it as you wish. I have grown rather fond of the way it sounds when you cry it out in the morning."

Her cheeks flushed, and she found herself suddenly battling away memories of her recent dreams. She turned away from Cruce and walked along the edge of the shade.

Subject change. Going to pretend he didn't say that...pretend it's not true.

"Where is the queen now?" she asked, almost managing a normal tone.

"She relocated her court many years ago. It is my hope that she perished in the process."

Sophie stopped and faced him again. "Harsh, considering you were both trying to use each other, and it was *you* who stabbed *her* in the back."

"Harsh?" He rose into a vaguely humanoid form and leaned toward her; he nearly vanished in the sunlight. "Harsh is what you see now. What she did to me. It was within her rights, within her power, to destroy me and lay claim to my realm. To end it there. Instead, she cursed me to *this* for eternity. Cursed me to watch my forest dwindle around me, powerless to protect it as I once did, cursed me to an endless hunger for *life* that drives me to destroy that which I was meant to guard!"

His voice had risen with every word, and his closeness was menacing despite his insubstantiality. To her shame, Sophie cringed back, ducking down and lifting her arms to protect herself from the barrage of fists that would undoubtedly follow.

Her heart thundered in her chest, her breath was suddenly strained, and her skin tingled with the threat of an impending panic attack.

The fall breeze rustled the leaves overhead and scattered those already littering the ground. Seconds passed, and nothing happened. He didn't strike her, didn't leap upon her, didn't suck the life out of her. Trembling, she lowered her arms to see him pressed against the wall of the house, his shadows squeezed into a narrow shape.

"My anger is not your burden to bear," he said, his voice as soft as the breeze. "I broke my oath to the fae queen long ago. I will not break my oath to you."

Sophie raised her head and straightened, folding her arms across her chest and tucking her hands beneath them to hide their trembling. She inhaled deeply and released the breath slowly, repeating the action several times as she willed herself to calm.

"Is…is there a way to break the curse?" she asked quietly.

"You are cold," he said, moving toward the far end of the porch. "You should return to your dwelling."

Sophie frowned. She hesitantly approached the porch steps and climbed them, stopping when she reached the top. "I'm sorry. I didn't mean to make it sound like your suffering doesn't matter."

"You need not apologize to me, Sophie." He rose from the floorboards and drifted toward her, a prowling beast one moment, an antlered humanoid the next. Extending an arm, he settled his palm on her cheek. It was cold, but it stirred a heat within her that she'd never felt before he'd come into her life.

She craved more of his touch. Her eyelids fluttered as something flowed through her; something powerful, something soul-deep, something that pulled her closer to him.

"Go warm yourself by your fire," Cruce said, his entire form shuddering. "I will not wander far."

Sophie was unable to form words, unable to move.

He withdrew his hand and retreated. An instant later, he was gone, dissipating like smoke carried off by the wind. Only then was the spell broken.

She shook off her daze and, after another glance at the woods, went back inside.

It was a struggle to go about her usual routine for the remainder of the day; she couldn't focus. She found herself erasing and rewriting sentences repeatedly, constantly dissatisfied with the results, and finally gave up and called Kate. There was no answer.

Unwilling to return to writing—at the rate she'd been going, she'd only end up slamming her head into the keyboard in frustration—she resumed her research on fae and spirits. The search engine offered millions of results; information from folklore, pop culture, paranormal romance and urban fantasy books, and countless other sources. She was certain some of it was accurate, but how could she know which was right?

All she had to go off was whatever Cruce decided to tell her, and he'd already admitted that he could lie.

She paused her research when evening came. She hadn't felt Cruce's presence at all since he'd departed. Strangely...she missed it; the feeling of being watched had become familiar to her, a silent reminder that someone, some*thing*, was here for her. That seemed an unhealthy way to think of it, but she couldn't deny that his presence made her feel less alone.

He said he wouldn't wander far. He's out there. He's just...giving me space.

After eating dinner, she spent a few more hours surfing the net, looking up fairy myths and curses, discovering nothing but conflicting information. Discouraged, she took a quick shower and went to bed.

She lay there for a long while, tossing and turning, until she finally ended up on her side, facing the window with its drawn curtains. She glared at it and clenched her jaw. The urge to go and open the curtains was a silly one. It wouldn't help her sleep. She just needed to stop her mind from running at a thousand miles an hour and *relax*.

After a few minutes, she sighed heavily, slipped out of bed, and threw the curtains open. Light from the moon and stars cast her room in a silver glow. She scanned the shadows outside, seeking Cruce. Though she saw no sign of him, she knew, somehow, he was out there.

Climbing back into bed, she pulled the cover up to her chest and lay facing the window. It wasn't until she was succumbing to sleep and her eyes were drifting shut that a dark shadow moved in front of the window, peering in with eyes like glittering stars.

CHAPTER SEVEN

"CRUCE?" Sophie called as she stepped onto the porch the next morning. Adjusting the strap of her purse over her shoulder, she turned and locked the door. When she was done, she scanned the tree line for movement. "You around, Cruce?"

There was no response.

Keys dangling in hand, she walked to her car. "Must be doing foresty things, like lording over the trees and squirrels." Sophie paused and snickered at the mental image her words produced. Shaking her head, she opened the door, slid into the driver's seat, and tossed her purse down beside her.

The drive into town was uneventful, allowing her a bit of leeway to enjoy the lovely scenery. She was going to be sad when the trees were bare, but she was sure the winter would bring its own unique beauty when it came; how would everything look with a layer of pristine white draped over it?

She stopped at the post office to check her PO box. There was a bright yellow envelope inside with familiar handwriting on the front. Smiling, Sophie pulled it out, tore it open, and withdrew the card, which had a glittery sun on the front. She ran a fingertip over Kate's looping script as she read the heart-felt message inside, and her day was instantly brightened.

There was gift card included inside, and the sticky note stuck to its front said *Spruce up the place! XOXO.* Sophie tucked it all carefully into her purse and closed her box.

After dropping Kate's birthday card into the drop box, Sophie went outside and dug her phone out from the bottom of her bag. She opened Facetime and tapped Kate's name. Her gaze wandered as it rang.

There were a surprising number of people out and about; some were walking dogs, others were accompanying young children who were excitedly taking in the Halloween decorations. Sophie couldn't help but smile. She hoped to reclaim some of that innocent excitement for herself. Cars rolled down the main street slowly, most of them seemingly respectful of the twenty-miles-per-hour speed limit within the town proper.

Her smile slipped when Kate didn't accept the call after far too many rings. She switched over to a regular call and waited. Kate's voicemail answered after the sixth ring.

"Hey Kate," Sophie said after the beep, "it's me! I wanted to hear your voice and thank you for the card. Just picked it up from the post office. Call me, okay?"

Unease filled her as she pressed *end*. What if Tyler had found out Kate was keeping watch on him? What if he found out Kate knew where Sophie was staying?

Would he hurt her? Had he already?

No. No, we're not going to play that game right now.

Kate was just busy. She wasn't sitting around all hours of the day, twiddling her thumbs and eagerly awaiting Sophie's call. She had a busy, demanding job and was living a life of her own, a life that now included a new guy. Kate deserved happiness. She didn't need to carry Sophie's burdens.

But no matter how many times Sophie tried to reassure herself, she still worried for her friend.

She hopped back into the car and made a quick stop at the grocery store for a few necessities. She hadn't planned on buying anything extra, but a piece of wall décor caught her eye —she knew she had to buy it the moment she saw it, and a smile played upon her lips when she thought about how Cruce would react to it.

There was still no Cruce when she arrived home. She gathered her grocery bags and swept her gaze over the woods as she walked to the front door. Once she'd put everything away, she headed back outside, checked for him again, and went back to the car to lift the large, metal piece of décor out of the trunk.

Back on the porch, she studied the exterior wall; there were several screws and nails protruding from it, some rusted with age. The pair of nails just over her eye level to the right of the front door seemed perfectly placed. She lifted the metal piece, settling the top of its outer circle on the nails, and stepped back to admire it. The black metal gleamed with reflected light. It depicted a tree enclosed in a circle, its roots and branches stretching wide in graceful, sweeping lines, and it looked perfect in its new spot.

"What is this?" Cruce asked from beside her.

Sophie jumped, a hand flying to her chest as she turned to him. He was a smoky column of shadow, resembling a tall man in a long, dark cloak. "You *have* to stop doing that!"

"Perhaps you should be more aware of your surroundings," he replied. She swore she heard a smirk in his voice.

Shaking her head, she motioned toward the piece. "What do you think?"

"What is it?" he asked again.

Sophie stared at him blankly. "A tree."

Though his form didn't seem to move, his eyes—barely visible in the daylight —turned to her. "Such symbols are often used as wards, but I sense no magic from this item. What is its *purpose?*"

"To look nice. And...it reminded me of you," she said, returning her attention to the art as her cheeks warmed in embarrassment. "You said you were the guardian spirit of this forest, so I figured this was perfect to hang here to, you know, show everyone else that this cabin is part of that." She shrugged. "Even if I'm the only one who knows what it means, I like that its here."

Cruce leaned closer to the metal tree and released a low hum. "Now that I know its meaning, I find my appreciation of it has increased."

Sophie smiled at him. "Really? You like it, then?"

"I do."

His touch settled on her calf, gentle and cold through her pants, and slowly trailed up.

A thrill spiraled through her, and she gasped softly. "Cruce..."

"Yes, Sophie?" He brushed the backside of her knee.

She hadn't realized just how sensitive that spot was until he stroked it. Her core pulsed, and liquid heat flooded her. How could so small, so light, so insignificant a touch have such a profound effect on her?

Some rational part of her brain urged her to say something, to stop him, to remind him of the boundaries she'd set, but she couldn't get the words past her lips. She'd said no groping; could it be argued that this didn't fall under that stipulation? This was a caress, seductive and sensual, but was there anything overtly sexual about it?

He shifted closer and raised a shadowy hand to run his fingers from her cheekbone to her jaw. "I have walked this forest for many thousands of years, and yet your beauty is unique to me. I have never seen its like. You surpass all I have ever known, Josephine Davis."

Her heartbeat quickened as she stared into his eyes. They beckoned her to give in, and for an instant they seemed the only light in a vast sea of darkness, her only hope for salvation. She tilted her face up toward him, eyelids growing heavy.

Cruce dipped toward her only to abruptly turn away and withdraw his shadows.

Sophie stumbled forward; she hadn't realized that she'd been leaning into his touch. Regaining her balance, she stepped back, slightly dazed from the euphoria their brief contact had created.

"What's wrong?" she asked.

"Humans have entered my domain," he replied. "I must ensure they mean my forest no harm."

His shadows collapsed upon themselves, turning into a pool of darkness that darted off the porch and out of her perception. She lifted her eyes, scanning the trees beyond her driveway. She thought she saw *something* moving between them...but it was too difficult to tell in the daylight.

Sophie released a long, slow breath. Her body thrummed with arousal; it had built so swiftly, so easily, under his touch.

Not even a day had passed since their agreement, and she'd already allowed him to affect her so thoroughly. Was she ever going to learn? His words didn't have to be genuine, and the more she accepted them at face value, the more vulnerable she was to hurt. Sophie had vowed to herself that she'd never allow another man to have so much power over her, and yet here she was, falling under Cruce's spell. She was undeniably, irresistibly drawn to him. Everything within her seemed to crave his nearness, his touch, his voice.

That frightened her.

Sophie scanned the trees once more before entering the cabin. She'd make herself some lunch and find something to occupy her time—and, hopefully, her thoughts.

She called Kate on Facetime again, but there was still no answer. Her worry deepened. Kate should have received the voicemail, should've seen the missed calls.

Carrying her laptop to the sofa, Sophie sat down and opened

the file for her work in progress. The words flowed easily this time. She lost herself in the story; part of her recognized that the turn it had taken was heavily influenced by Cruce—the mysterious hero watching over the heroine, safeguarding her— but she refused to acknowledge it outright.

Whatever she hoped for with him, real life never worked out the way things did in books and movies.

By the time she came up for air, it was well past five o'clock, and her stomach was growling; she'd forgotten about lunch. She devoured a bowl of soup and stepped outside after cleaning up. The sky was darkening; violet, magenta, and gold stained the western horizon. She inhaled the fresh air appreciatively.

"Cruce?" she called, watching for movement.

No answer.

When she called his name again and there was still no response, she made her way toward the forest. After sitting for most the of afternoon, she needed a walk to stretch her legs. It had nothing to do with being anxious to see Cruce. It didn't. She'd be sure to stay on the trail this time and turn back well before full dark. Despite her last woodland experience, she wasn't afraid.

Was that Cruce's doing? Had his oath granted her courage?

Was it foolish to take him at his word?

As someone who'd earned a living by using words to create fantastical, imaginary characters, worlds, and stories, she should've known how empty they could be. By themselves, words were nothing; they were empty and hollow. How many times had Tyler professed his love and promised never to hurt her again? How many times had she made herself believe him?

Words—*promises*—were only as good as the person, as the *actions*, behind them.

And Cruce was not Tyler. As frightening as Cruce seemed, as monstrous as he appeared, the true monster was Sophie's husband.

She paused at one of the larger trees to touch the green, spongy moss on its trunk; it felt like brushing her fingertips over velvet.

A rustling sound caught her attention. She stepped away from the tree and turned her head to listen. The sound came again, accompanied by movement in the fallen leaves to her right. She approached the source slowly. A moment later, she noticed a rabbit, half-buried in the foliage, staring up at her. Its long ears were raised, and its wide, dark eyes gleamed with fear.

"Aww. Hey," she said softly.

The rabbit twitched as though it meant to jump but remained in place.

"Shh. I won't hurt you, little guy."

Crouching, she tentatively reached toward the animal. The shivering rabbit's sides heaved with rapid breaths. It flinched when she settled her hand lightly on its back and ran her palm over its fur.

"Are you hurt?"

Despite its obvious terror, the creature didn't flee. Sophie frowned and carefully slipped her hands around the rabbit, meaning to pick it up, but stilled when her fingers touched something wet. She lifted a hand to see a smear of blood on her thumb.

She brushed aside the surrounding leaves to reveal an old, rusted coil-spring trap. Her eyes widened. The trap was closed around one of the rabbit's hind legs. The fur around it was matted with bright blood.

"Oh my God," she whispered.

She couldn't guess how long the animal had been trapped, but its muted reactions suggested it had been here for hours, at least—long enough to exhaust itself.

How many other traps were out here? Sophie had wandered blindly through the woods just the other day; what if she'd stepped on one? This could've been *her* foot.

Kneeling, she cleared away the remaining leaves and examined the trap. She kept her movements slow to avoid frightening the rabbit any further. It jumped as though attempting to escape, tearing more of the flesh around its wound.

"Shh. I'm going to get you out of this, okay?"

It took Sophie a few attempts to figure out how the trap's mechanism worked, and her heart broke when the rabbit released a series of high, distressed sounds. She continued to speak to it calmly as she finally pried the jaws open.

Once its leg was free, she gathered the rabbit in her arms and held it securely against her chest, ignoring the blood on her hands and shirt; another load of laundry didn't matter compared to this animal's needless suffering.

"Let's take you home and get you fixed up. How's that sound?"

Sophie crooned to the animal, gently scratching behind its ears. Surprisingly, it seemed to relax, nuzzling itself against her chest. "You can be my new little friend."

CRUCE SPED BETWEEN THE TREES, passing over ground both ever-changing and ever-familiar. His forest was but a single facet of nature, a reflection of it cast on a scale so tiny in comparison to the cosmos that it was made insignificant in the grand scheme, but it was *his*. Here, there was balance—chaos and order, growth and entropy, life and death, all keeping each other in check.

At least when outside forces did not interfere.

Unfortunately, humans had become both more commonplace and more destructive over the last few centuries. Many seemed to view nature as a thing to use as they wished, a dangerous attitude when combined with their general carelessness and irreverence. Cruce had devoured the essences of many humans since he was cursed. He believed most had been deserving of their fates.

He could not tolerate those who would inflict undue harm upon his forest.

Soon enough, he heard them—a group of male mortals, conversing loudly. Cruce remained low to the ground until he was closer to the humans and then drew himself into the shaded hollow of a tree to watch them.

Four mortals were walking through the woods, dressed in a combination of earthy, natural colors and bright orange vests and hats. Cruce had seen the combination before; many of the hunters who'd come to his realm in the last few decades wore similar attire. Each man wore a backpack, and they all had guns slung over their shoulders. Two were carrying a large red box with a white lid together, one on each side.

"How much farther, Bill?" asked one of the men.

"Not much, Kev. Almost there," another—presumably *Bill* —replied.

"Why do we always gotta hike so damn far?" asked one of the men carrying the red box.

"Why do you have to ask the same question every time, Joe?" Bill stopped and turned to Joe, frowning. "We don't want anyone to bother us, right? Farther we are from the roads, less chance we have of running into anyone who might ask questions about what we bag out here."

"Would you just shut up and walk?" said the man holding the other side of the container. "Otherwise I might as well be carrying the cooler alone."

"I'll *make* you carry it yourself if you're gonna be an asshole, Matt," Joe snapped.

Their conversation continued in that fashion as they walked; they belittled one another often and seemed to have little patience for each other. Cruce followed alongside them, thinning himself as much as possible to avoid rustling the vegetation and betraying his presence; the diminishing effects of the daylight were for once a boon.

The humans often spoke of things he didn't fully understand —tags and licensing, *dee-you-eyes*, parole officers—but he didn't need to understand. Their nearness stirred his hunger.

Their life force was nothing compared to the taste he'd had of Sophie's, and yet it tempted him. The sense of hollowness inside deepened, and his need strengthened. They could satisfy his hunger for days. Their deaths would allow him to focus solely upon Sophie, perhaps even until All Hallows Eve.

He held himself back; it would require too much of his reduced strength to drain all four mortals while the sun was up, and they'd not yet shown themselves to be a threat to his realm. Hunters could often serve to correct the balance in the forest, thinning the populations of beasts that had been allowed to rampantly reproduce. It would weaken Cruce in the short term, but ultimately led to a stronger forest by safeguarding against overfeeding.

Of course, that overpopulation was largely due to humans hunting many of the forest's natural predators to extinction, so he felt no obligation to give *any* of them the benefit of the doubt.

Soon, the mortals found a clear patch of ground and established a crude campsite. They built a haphazard fire, assembled two mismatched tents, and took silver-canned beverages out of the red container. All four drank greedily, tossing the empty cans onto the forest floor around them.

Cruce's mood darkened. He did not appreciate the trash humans often left behind, but such was not grounds enough for death. He'd witnessed many of them respectfully gather their leavings and haul them away when they departed in the past.

The mortals grew louder and increasingly obnoxious as the empty cans piled up. They hurled insults, laughed at each other's expense, and seemed on the verge of violence on several occasions. Joe produced a small white bottle at one point and squirted some of its contents into the fire. The flames roared and leapt high, nearly engulfing Matt, who'd been leaning close. Joe seemed greatly amused by the situation; it took Kev and Bill's combined efforts to pull Matt off him.

The fools would burn down half the forest if they continued with such recklessness. Cruce had never been so eager for the approaching twilight.

Surprisingly, the mortals quieted down after the altercation. One of them tugged a container from his bag and walked out of the campsite. Cruce followed him and watched as the man entered a nearby clearing and opened the lid to shake out fine seed from the container, scattering it across the ground. When he was done, he returned to his companions, and all four gathered their guns.

Glancing once more at their still-blazing fire, Cruce trailed the hunters as they left their camp. They took position not far from the scattered seed, crouching together behind a fallen log with their weapons propped up on the wood. One of the men laughed, only to be hushed by his companions.

Cruce crept closer to the humans and eased himself into a shady patch. Their carelessness was infuriating—his shadows roiled, resisting his efforts to hold a consistent shape—but the late afternoon sun was still too bright to act. He was in no state to chase terrified mortals through the woods after sucking the life from the first. In fact, he would much rather have returned to Sophie, forgetting these humans altogether. They would likely prove harmless; most of them did, in the end.

But he could not shake his foreboding about this group.

The humans were surprisingly quiet as they waited; the sun crept closer and closer to the western horizon, but its movement wasn't nearly fast enough for Cruce.

He sensed the birds arriving before he saw them—a few curious chickadees at first, but their numbers swelled as they excitedly chirped about the abundant food. Before long, crows and mockingbirds had arrived to partake in the feast, along with a family of cardinals.

"Can we start yet?" Joe asked.

"Soon," Bill said. "Got more coming."

Kev turned his head toward Bill. "Same scoring as usual?"

"Yeah. Double points if you bring them down alive."

"Aim for the wings," Matt said with a grin.

Sophie called Cruce's name at that moment; it coursed through him, tingling and powerful, compelling him to go to her. But he sensed no distress in her call, no command. He shoved the sensation aside. Though he didn't want to spend any more time away from her, he had to address this situation first. He needed to learn if the hunters' conversation meant what he thought.

Any doubts he'd harbored about the appropriate fates for these mortals were crushed when Bill's signal began their *game*. All four men fired their guns at the birds, the weapons' blasts combining into one thunderous boom that echoed through the trees. Cruce felt the damage done to several of the birds. With startled calls, the rest of the creatures took wing.

The mortals hurried to their feet and fired rapidly into the scattering birds. The booming shots nearly drowned out the panicked avian cries.

The pain and terror of the animals crashed into Cruce and became his own for a fleeting moment. His rage swept in immediately afterward. He surged forward, directly into the sunlight; it did not slow his advance, but he felt immediately *lesser*, as though it was his own life force being drained. Growling inwardly, he retreated to the shade beneath the canopy.

The mortals stopped shooting. For a few moments, the only sounds were the fading echo of the final gunshot and the distant calls of fleeing birds. Several feathers drifted lazily in the air to land amidst the fallen leaves. On the ground, the few fallen birds still clinging to life flapped their wings frantically in vain attempts to escape. They were surrounded by lifeless bodies.

One of the mortals laughed. This time, the others joined in.

"Three," Matt said, "with two still kicking."

Kev grunted. "Two and one for me."

"Four and two," muttered Bill.

"Ten and three!" Joe declared.

"Oh, bullshit," Matt and Kev said in unison.

"You lying rat bastard," Bill grumbled.

Without another glance at the still-twitching birds, the humans walked toward their campsite. They made no attempt to collect either the cylinders expelled by their weapons and or the animals they'd killed.

Cruce maintained his position until the sun finally dipped behind the trees and cast long shadows across the forest floor. He glided over the open ground, stretching his form to encompass the wounded birds. Their mangled wings and bloodied feathers were not a new sight to him, but the carnage struck him deeply because of its pointlessness.

Death for amusement was an abomination in Cruce's eyes. Nature could be cruel, could be cold and unforgiving, but everything served its purpose in the natural order.

Cruce drained the lingering life energies from the injured birds, ending their suffering. Though the power was slight, it rushed through him, pairing with the deepening twilight to strengthen his form, granting him a sense of solidness he'd not experienced in weeks. He gathered himself into a pool of darkness and moved toward the human camp.

Smoke from their fire billowed into the evening air, and its flames burned higher than before. The mortals were gathered around it, laughing and talking boisterously, sipping their canned drinks.

"We should get some food going before it's too dark," one of them said.

Vengeance and ravenousness swirled inside Cruce in a raging torrent of fury. As he neared the mortals, he shaped himself into a semblance of the body he'd possessed in his natural state. He pushed himself up with shadowy arms, lifted legs formed of darkness out of the shadows pooled on the ground, and stalked toward his prey.

"Later," another human said. "We got plenty of time."

"Hey, what the fu—"

The human sitting on the other side of the fire, facing Cruce, scrambled backward with wide eyes. His companions were slower to react; the man nearest Cruce was twisting to look behind himself as the forest spirit pounced.

Cruce fell upon the seated human, wrapping him in shadow, and drew in the man's frantic, terror-fused life force. The other humans shouted and fumbled for their weapons even as they scrambled away.

They fired their guns. Projectiles blasted through Cruce, unhindered by his insubstantial form, and struck the human in his grasp. The mortal's life force dissipated abruptly; he was dead. Growling, Cruce launched himself at the next-closest human. The man stumbled back and fired his gun.

More projectiles harmlessly passed through Cruce. An instant later, a mortal cried out in pain behind him.

Enveloping the second human, Cruce pulled on the man's life force; the inhalation of another being's essence was the closest he could come to breathing. The human screamed and writhed, but his struggles were in vain. Cruce felt himself swelling with new energy as the final, rattling breath escaped his victim's throat.

He turned toward the remaining mortals. The injured man was sitting on the ground with blood flowing from his gut, desperately manipulating his gun to load new projectiles. The other—Bill—stared at Cruce for a moment before sprinting away.

The air was redolent with the smell of their fear. Cruce relished it; terror added a unique, satisfying flavor to their essences, a flavor he'd come to enjoy over the long years. He no longer knew if that enjoyment was a product of his curse or the darkness he'd always harbored.

Cruce altered his shape to extend black wings to either side and charged after Bill. Thrusting his antlered head forward, he opened his long beak and loosed a blood-curdling call—the cry of a hunting falcon, the caw of an angry crow, the roar of a beast that would no longer tolerate disrespect in its own domain.

Bill glanced over his shoulder and screamed before his foot caught on a root. He tumbled, crashing over fallen leaves, and scurried onto his back as Cruce leapt atop him.

Fear-tinged life force flowed into Cruce, sweetened by Bill's agonized death cries. As the fresh surge of strength filled Cruce, he raked shadowy claws across Bill's torso, shredding clothing and flesh alike. The consumed energy and the nearness of All Hallows Eve produced a rush of power in him like he hadn't known in so long; this was as close as he'd been to his old self in nearly two centuries.

And he hungered for *more*.

Casting aside Bill's corpse, Cruce assumed the shape of a huge wolf and prowled back into the camp. He followed the blood trail on the carpet of leaves to find the final human, Joe, crawling away.

Joe twisted to look over his shoulder. "Oh, no. God, please, no!" He struggled forward, clawing at the ground, his words descending into senseless, panicked blubbering.

Cruce pressed his paws onto the human's back, pinning the man in place. As he leaned forward, his paws changed, lengthening into talons that curled around the mortal's torso and sank into tender rib flesh.

Joe writhed in pain. Cruce wrapped a tendril of shadow around the man's head, forcing it back. When Joe screamed,

Cruce poured malleable shadow down his throat, cutting off the terrified cry. He drained the human's essence from the inside.

Cruce rose after Joe's body—as unimportant to the Lord of the Forest as the birds had been to these hunters—sagged lifelessly to the ground. He would leave them for the forest to claim through scavengers and decay, just as they had left the animals they'd killed.

He assumed his old shape, the shape that could be mistaken for human on dark, gloomy nights, and could *almost* feel it— could almost feel powerful muscles moving beneath golden skin, could almost feel the reassuring weight of mighty antlers, could almost feel fiery blood flowing through his veins. The very power enabling him to hold his shadows in this shape was so overwhelming it threatened to tear him apart.

He clenched his fists and raised them above his waist, pushing to *feel*, to *be*, but he knew it was beyond him. The curse would not allow it.

Only Sophie could grant him anything close to the sensations he craved. Only contact with her could give him warmth, pleasure, meaning.

Cruce turned his back on the fallen mortals and darted through the trees toward Sophie, sped on by the growing twilight.

CHAPTER EIGHT

THOUGH NIGHT HAD NOT YET FULLY FALLEN when Cruce arrived at the cabin, it was dark enough that the lights from within cast a gentle glow on the surrounding grounds. It seemed a strange contrast to the raging fire the hunters had built; this was a controlled light, a welcoming light, a soothing light, and he was drawn to it.

He recalled the way she'd reacted to his touch before he'd gone to investigate the new human presence in his realm; she hadn't been pulling away from him, she'd been leaning into him as though wanting for *more*—just as he'd almost been unable to pull away from her. For those fleeting moments, they'd been experiencing the same thing. They'd been *craving* the same thing.

As he approached the porch, he spied her in the kitchen with her back to the window. His excitement increased; he was barely able to contain the energy brimming within him.

He watched her silently for a moment. Her shoulders and arms moved as she worked on something in front of her, something he couldn't see. His gaze roamed over her body; the curves of her hips and backside, which swayed subtly as she shifted her weight from one foot to the other, and the graceful length of her neck. Her plaited auburn hair hung down the center of her back. He wanted to loosen it, to run his fingers through those silken tresses, to feel their softness. He wanted to feel *her* softness against him. But, no matter how substantial he felt, he could not truly have that experience yet.

A few more days...

He glided up the steps and stopped in front of the window on the kitchen side.

"Sophie," he called.

She turned her head and looked in his direction, but he doubted she could see him through the reflections on the inside of the glass. Her brow furrowed. "Cruce?"

The sound of his true name from her lips sent a thrill through him.

"Come to me, Josephine Davis," he beckoned.

"Just a second." She turned her attention back to her task, slowly raising her arms and lowering them. She grabbed a small towel beside her and wiped her hands with it before tossing it back on the table.

Cruce drifted to the entryway to await her. Several moments later, she opened the interior door, spilling light onto the porch. Though he was directly in its path, the sense of diminishment was minimal; he'd never drained so much life force in so short a time, even at the heights of his ravenousness.

His gaze traveled over her again, and he was blasted by sudden alarm—the front of her shirt was stained with blood.

"What happened?" he demanded, his shadows rising, growing, darkening. "Where are you harmed?"

Sophie's eyes widened. "What do you mean? I'm not—"

He pressed himself to the screen door, seeping through it partially to roil against the invisible barrier marking the threshold. "You are covered in blood, Josephine."

She looked down at herself. "Oh! It's not mine, really. I just haven't had a chance to change and clean up yet."

Cruce ran a set of shadowy claws through the air, brushing the line he could not cross, longing to touch her. To assure himself that she was well. Her scent was by far the strongest he could perceive; in his physical form, he could have distinguished the smell of blood by the species from which it had originated, but now he could barely detect it at all. "If not yours, who does it belong to?"

"Hold on."

She turned and walked into the kitchen.

Frustration mixed with Cruce's confusion; he could not follow her, and despite seeming comfortable with him, she'd not deigned to invite him inside. Why were his emotions so volatile? He'd never felt as much concern as he had at the sight of Sophie splattered with blood. The wellbeing of a single mortal shouldn't have been of any importance to the Lord of the Forest; countless millions of humans had lived and died over the course of his existence, and not one had ever drawn his attention for more than a fleeting instant.

She returned a few moments later carrying a brown box. Turning, she pushed the screen door open with her hip. Cruce moved backward as she stepped onto the porch.

"I went on a walk earlier, and I came across this little guy." She lowered the box and carefully tilted it to reveal a small brown rabbit nestled in a thin blanket, a bandage around one of its hind legs. Sophie frowned. "He was caught in an old trap. His leg got pretty torn up, but I don't think anything's broken."

Cruce extended a tendril of shadow, sliding it toward the creature. The rabbit, nose twitching, pressed itself against the side of box. The animals of Cruce's domain feared him; he could not fault them for it, as much as it pained him to be reminded of the fact. He was a thing unnatural to them. A predator that preyed upon *anything* living.

He touched the rabbit gently, running the tendril across its fur. The animal trembled. Its leg was not broken, as she'd guessed, but the rabbit had suffered. And its suffering, like that of so many of his creatures, had been the result of human carelessness.

His shadows roiled, and it took no small amount of effort to bring them under control. Bill and his hunters rose to the forefront of Cruce's mind—their willful cruelty, the joy and amusement they'd found in the suffering of other creatures, their disregard for his forest. Fury ignited within him.

But he swallowed it, tamped it back down, as he lifted his gaze to Sophie. She was not like them. She was the reason to put aside his anger, to ease himself. "And you rescued this animal. You have tended to it."

"Well, yeah. I wasn't going to just leave him there to suffer."

Her compassion was refreshing after what he'd witnessed; it served as a welcome contrast not only to the cruelty of the other mortals, but to the vengeance Cruce had enacted. Life was a simple thing to take. To end. Helping another creature survive, however, was often far harder. It would've taken Sophie less effort to break the rabbit's neck and be done—or simply walk away and leave it to its fate—than to free it, bring it home, and treat its wound.

Such acts were beyond his capability now. Thanks to his curse, he could only *take*; he couldn't give to his forest and its creatures. Once, he would've been able to heal the rabbit. In his current state, he could only have stolen its life force.

The very life force thrumming against his extended tendril; panicked, ephemeral, tempting.

He withdrew from the creature abruptly, shifting his focus back to Sophie. "You have done more than most would, Josephine."

She looked down at the rabbit. "It's...easy to ignore when others are suffering. Easier to pretend that nothing's going on, because that way we don't have to get involved. But there *are* people who are willing to help. They're not always easy to find, but they're out there."

"Like your Kate?"

"Yeah, like Kate." She moved away, sat on an old chair on the far end of the porch, and settled the box in her lap. The wooden chair creaked beneath her weight.

Cruce glided closer to her, pausing in the patch of shadow between the open door and the window. "What did he do to you, Sophie?"

Sophie laughed humorlessly without looking at him. "It'd be easier to ask what he *didn't* do to me." She reached into the box and petted the rabbit. There was a pained crease between her brows, and her lips were turned down. She stared off into the distance with a blankness in her eyes Cruce didn't care for.

He slid a tendril of shadow to her, trailing it over her ankle. Her warmth was greater than ever, and he could *almost* feel the texture of her sock. "Tell me, Josephine Davis."

She glanced at the shadow caressing her ankle before shifting her eyes to him for several moments. Finally, she sighed and dropped her gaze to the rabbit.

"Tyler is a good-looking guy. He has an air about him, a charisma, that draws people in. And there I was, sitting alone in the same ole coffee shop, in the same ole spot I did everyday while I was writing, and all of the sudden...his attention was on me. I was shocked that he took any interest, that he chose *me* out of all the women there. He flirted with me, and he came back over the next few days. He seemed so interested in me, in my life. That felt so good that I never...never realized what he was actually doing."

Cruce had been attracted to Sophie from the beginning; she had her own draw that she didn't seem aware of, a power beyond her control. He guessed that it wasn't that draw which had lured Tyler in, however. "What was he doing?"

"Targeting me. And I was so gullible, too. I let his charming smile, sweet words, and attentiveness break down whatever meager defenses I had left." She tilted her head, and a loose tendril of hair drifted down to brush her cheek. "I had just lost my parents a few months before, I had no close friends, no other living relatives, and my work is very solitary by nature. I went to that coffee shop all the time, but I never *talked* to anyone. It was just... I had felt too isolated at home, after my parents passed, so I went there just to not feel so alone.

"He picked up on that quickly. I had no one, and I was a lot more vulnerable than I realized. If I had had a friend to tell me that things were moving too quickly, that something didn't seem right about him, someone to show me the signs, I might have made very different choices. But he swept me off my feet so quickly, I didn't even realize I was falling.

"We married three months later. It felt like a whirlwind romance, but in hindsight I understand that we moved that fast so I wouldn't have time to see through the cracks in the mask he presented to the world. I never really got to know him. He'd made it all about me. And he didn't show his true colors right away. In some sick way, he loved me, cherished me...but as a *possession*, not as a partner."

She shook her head and caught her lower lip between her teeth for a moment. "I think I knew on some level that things weren't quite right, but it was subconscious. I mean...I never even told him that I usually went by Sophie. I introduced myself as Josephine, and he started calling me Josie, and I just went with it. I figured it was...our *thing*, since he was the only one who called me that."

"Sophie is the name of your heart," Cruce said, echoing what he'd told her when they'd exchanged true names. "Why Sophie and not Josephine?"

"My parents always called me Sophie," she replied, a sad smile touching her lips as she briefly looked up at Cruce. "They said when I was really little I couldn't pronounce Josephine, that it always just came out as Sophie, and they thought it was so cute that it stuck. I loved it. And, you know…I'm glad I never told him. It's a piece of me that he'll never get to have. It's *mine*, the one thing he didn't take."

Cruce gave her ankle a gentle squeeze, eliciting a fresh wave of warmth. "Continue, Sophie."

"It wasn't long after we got married that he started to drop hints about me giving up writing. First it was about the money. He made a good salary, and we didn't *need* the money I was bringing in. When I repeatedly insisted that I enjoyed it and that I wanted to continue anyway, his tone started to change. It became about me writing smut, filth, and he couldn't tolerate a wife who imagined other men, who thought about sex with them.

"He forbade me from going to the coffee shop, and pretty soon that extended to almost anywhere. I wasn't allowed to go out alone because he didn't want me flirting with other men. It got to the point where if I so much as glanced at another man, Tyler's mood would swing, and he'd accuse me of contemplating infidelity. The only place I was allowed to go by myself was the grocery store while he was at work, but even then, he'd text or call me through the whole trip to make sure I wasn't doing anything he deemed *inappropriate*. But he'd always reel it back in afterward and explain that it was just because he loved me so much, because he wanted me safe. And even if I didn't quite buy that, I went along with it. For years."

Sophie shifted her hands down to the underside of the box, clenching its corners, but not before Cruce noticed their slight trembling.

He wound the tendril on her ankle farther up her leg as he shifted the rest of his shadows into place behind her chair and rose over her. He settled a shadowy hand on her shoulder, wishing for that last bit of feeling, for those missing sensations that seemed so *close*. She leaned slightly into his touch.

Cruce understood possessiveness. This forest was his, and he wanted *her* to be his, too. But possession was no guarantee of satisfaction. If Sophie wasn't happy... She'd be surviving, but not *alive*. Like a bird with clipped wings, confined forever to the ground even though its soul was meant to soar. All the beauty that shone from within her, all the light she carried in her heart, would eventually fade until it extinguished.

"One night," Sophie continued, "about five months after we got married, we went out with a few of his coworkers he was friendly with. I think Tyler wanted to show me off a little—it was okay when he wanted to do it, I guess. Anyway, I got dressed up, and we met his friends at a bar. Things were going well, and I was enjoying myself more than I had in a while. As much of a recluse as I'd been before, it was worse after I married Tyler, so it was nice to get out of the house, to be around people, just laughing and having fun.

"But one of his friends, Dan, kept engaging me in conversation. Tyler didn't seem to have a problem when I was talking to his coworkers' wives, and I didn't think anything of it. I smiled and chatted with Dan, not realizing how stiff Tyler was getting beside me, or how much he was drinking. Tyler jumped into the conversation often, trying to steer it away from anything that would involve me, but Dan was persistent. He kept returning his attention to me.

"I knew Tyler was...upset when he excused us from the table. He took my wrist," she curled her fingers into a fist, "and I remember how much it hurt. He squeezed *so* hard." She paused and slowly unclenched her hand. "He pulled me outside, into the parking lot. Away from the little group of people standing near the doors. He didn't yell. His rage was in his eyes, his tone, his body language. He accused me of flirting with Dan, said the way we looked at each other suggested we'd already gone behind his back.

"I denied everything. And I was angry, *so* damn angry. I'd

been having fun for the first time in a long while, just being a normal person, and I was hurt that he'd accuse me of all these horrible things. That he was so distrustful of me. I called him paranoid, and he...hit me."

She touched the tips of her fingers to the corner of her mouth. "It was the first time he'd ever done that. I was shocked, totally stunned. And so was he. He'd hit me hard enough that my teeth cut my lip, and a bit of blood dripped onto my white dress. My mouth tasted like iron, and I felt...sick.

"He dropped to his knees and threw his arms around me, holding me close, apologizing over and over again, telling me that he loved me, that he was sorry, and begged for my forgiveness. He swore he'd never do it again. And I...I believed him. I forgave him. I could *smell* how much he'd been drinking, and told myself it was an accident. He loved me, of course he'd never hurt me on purpose. I was his wife."

Sophie shook her head. Her voice had grown huskier, and when she sniffed, unshed tears gleamed in her eyes. "That was the first time, but it was only a little taste of what was to come. He drank a lot more often after that night, and alcohol brought out the worst in him...but even when he wasn't drinking, I always seemed to do *something* that displeased him. I think he began to like the power he had over me. That he could bring me to heel, that I'd cower at his feet, whimpering, and do whatever he wanted to avoid another outburst. And he'd usually beg for forgiveness afterward, sometimes giving me little gifts, and I always said I forgave him. I didn't know what else to do, and I... think I died a little more on the inside every time I let him get away with it. And then..."

Tears spilled down her cheeks. She wiped the back of her hand across her face before dropping it to clutch the box again. "I denied him sex. I couldn't...couldn't bring myself to be intimate with him anymore. He was crushing me, killing me from the inside out. His touch was hurtful and sickening, especially when he caressed me as though he loved me. I knew by then that I'd never really loved him. I'd never really *known* him. And that night when I said *no*, when I drew away from him…he forced me. He put his hand around my throat and raped me."

Cruce's rage at the hunter's actions earlier was nothing compared to what roared through him in reaction to Sophie's story. It was anger like he'd never experienced, beyond what he'd felt even when he'd been cursed, beyond anything he could have felt on his own behalf. To have had a being so precious as Sophie and to have treated her so terribly, with such undue cruelty and malice, was unthinkable to him.

Perhaps it was part of why her life force burned so brightly. Part of why she was so appealing to him. Her survival had strengthened her in many ways, he did not doubt that, but it had also left her with these scars, had left her to carry this terrible, crushing burden on her own.

"Cruce?" she asked uncertainly. "You're…you're getting colder."

He withdrew his touch from her abruptly and returned to the shadows between window and doorway. He didn't want to hear more, but he *had* to listen. Had to know. "I am sorry, Sophie. Continue."

She stared at him for a time, her tear-filled eyes sparkling with reflected light. "Why do you want to know?"

"Because in sharing this part of yourself, you will allow me to carry some of your burden," he replied.

"What about your burden? Your curse? You still haven't told me how it can be broken."

"Finish your story, Josephine Davis."

She frowned, running her gaze over him before turning her face back to the rabbit. "That night taught me it was easier—less painful—to give in to him. And I think he craved that control. I think he was…*aroused* by my helplessness, by the damage he could inflict upon me without consequence. He hurt me often.

He treated the marks he left on my body like brands of owner-ship, proof that I was his. Welts from his belt, bruises from his hands, marks from his teeth. But he was the only one allowed to see them."

She released a shuddering breath. "Kate moved in across the street from us after we'd been together for a couple of years. She came to the house one day to introduce herself. Tyler was home, and he laid on that easy charm. He even introduced me to her. Once the door was closed, he told me that *he* was my only friend, and I wasn't to talk to that woman again. My place was at his side and nowhere else.

"About a week later, I was outside getting the mail out of the mail box, and Kate approached me. She was so warm and friendly, so bright and full of life. I couldn't imagine what I looked like in her eyes. I hardly recognized myself when I looked in the mirror. I excused myself as fast as I could and returned to the house. Kate never gave up though. She visited often, finding excuses to talk to me—bringing fresh picked flowers, cookies, a casserole, inviting me over for tea. And I *craved* her company so badly that I...I accepted it, even knowing what the consequences would be if Tyler found out.

"I did everything I could to keep our friendship secret. She works for an accounting firm, but they let her work from home pretty often, so I was able to visit with her while Tyler was away at work. I just had to make sure I left in time to have dinner ready for him when he came home. I never once spoke about her to Tyler, and I never said anything to her about the way he treated me. But...she knew. Even before she saw the bruising, I think she knew. And I was *terrified*. I made her promise not to tell anyone, not to call the police. I didn't know what Tyler would do if he found out.

"Then one day, he came home drunk. Drunker than I'd ever seen him. I had dinner on the table, warm and ready, I smiled and acted like the perfect wife, but... I don't know what happened. Maybe I flinched when he touched me, maybe he saw in my eyes how much I hated him and my life, or maybe I cooked the green beans a few minutes too long. For whatever reason, he snapped. He punched me in the stomach and accused me of *faking*, then hit me a few more times. He trashed the kitchen around me, throwing every plate and bowl of food I'd prepared across the room. Then I was his target again."

Her tears continued to flow, and her voice had grown so small. "By the time he sat down with his back against the wall and passed out with another bottle of booze in his hand—he'd tried to break it over my head, but it was tougher than he'd thought it would be—I was covered in blood. Every part of my body was in agony, and I was pretty sure I would die. I used what little strength I had to crawl out of the house and get to Kate's. I remember the feeling of the pavement digging into my palms and knees…it felt like broken glass, but it was just white noise against all the pain I was already in.

"Kate almost broke down when she opened her door and saw me. She helped me inside, locked the door, and called the police. They arrested Tyler, and I went to the hospital to recover for a few weeks.

"After that, I stayed with Kate, and we planned my escape. Thankfully, Tyler never knew about the bank account I'd had from before met, where my book royalties were deposited. Kate helped me find a good lawyer, helped me navigate the legal processes, and bought this cabin to rent out to me so there'd be no ownership trail for Tyler to follow. And…here I am. Hiding. Hoping to eventually regain what I lost…to start a new life."

Cruce raged for her, but there was much more than rage swirling within him. He mourned her stolen joy, felt her lingering pain, and yearned to heal the damage that had been wrought to her heart.

"I have never before wished to be able to leave the boundaries of my forest," he said softly, "but I do now."

Sophie raised her head and looked at him. "Why?"

"So I may find Tyler, rip him to shreds, and tear the life force from his body. I wish to make him suffer tenfold what you have suffered."

Her lips parted, and her eyes widened infinitesimally. She looked away from him. "That you've vowed to protect me is enough, Cruce." She lowered the box to her feet and reached inside to carefully cover the rabbit with the end of the blanket.

"No, it is not," Cruce said, moving closer to her. The strain of holding his form in check was immense. "He is the reason you fear. And he must pay for what he has taken from you. For what he has done to you."

Sophie leaned back and glanced down at herself—at the blood. She sighed and folded her hands in her lap. "It seems horrible to say this, but...that's the sweetest thing I've heard from a man in a long time." When she met his gaze again, she wore a faint, haunted smile.

Cruce stretched an arm toward her, cradling her cheek in his palm. He longed to touch her flesh to flesh, to soothe her, to caress her pain away. To provide her that simplest, most primal comfort. "Then the men in your life have ever been unworthy of you."

Her smile strengthened. She reached toward him and slipped a hand into his outer shadows, watching the dark, misty tendrils weave through her fingers. "Your turn. How can your curse be broken?"

"You need not concern yourself over my fate, Sophie."

Her brows lowered, and she frowned at him. "I told you my story. Now you tell me how to break your curse. An even trade, right?"

"That is not how this works."

"Yes it—"

"There is *nothing* for me to tell you," he growled.

She cringed, snapping her mouth shut, and a pang of regret

pierced him. His remorse strengthened when she withdrew her hand and leaned away from his touch.

"All curses can be broken. Each has a key. I do not know what will end my curse, nor do I know where to begin," he said, forcing his voice to a gentler tone. "The queen left my woods long ago, and there is no one left within my reach capable of puzzling it out."

"I'm sorry," she said. "I wish there was something I could do to help."

"You've already helped more than you can know." He sank lower and eased toward Sophie, looking up into her face. "Do not concern yourself over me. I will endure until nothing remains of my forest, with or without the curse."

"That's such a sad way to exist."

"My existence has contained little sorrow over the last several days, Josephine Davis." He brushed an inky tendril across her thigh.

Her legs parted slightly, and her breath quickened. She stared at him with dark eyes. The aroma of her arousal perfumed the air, mixing with her sweet lavender and vanilla scent, and Cruce pulled it into himself. He held onto it, absorbed it; he could *almost* taste it.

Her chest rose and fell rapidly, and heat emanated from her. She curled her fingers into the loose fabric of her shirt and twisted it.

"Cruce," she whispered.

Pinning her with his eyes, he shifted closer, running that wispy tendril higher to slip around her thigh. He moved his mouth to her ear. "Let me in, Sophie."

She gasped and leapt up. The chair scraped over the floorboards and teetered, nearly tipping over. Sophie threw a hand out to steady herself on the porch rail as she stumbled away. For several moments, she stared at him, wide-eyed and trembling. Did she fear him, or the way she reacted to him?

In a rush of motion, she snatched up the box and hurried past him, throwing the screen door open and darting inside.

Her sudden retreat caught Cruce off guard. He moved to follow her as the screen door slammed shut, pushing himself through only to be stopped by the invisible barrier at the threshold. Sophie adjusted her hold on the box to grasp the main door in one hand and turned to push it closed. She paused when her eyes met Cruce's.

"Let me in, Sophie," he repeated, voice husky with desire. He wanted to taste her, to touch her. He needed *all* of her.

She shook her head. "I can't."

Before he could ask *why*, she shut the door. There was a soft *thump* as she leaned against it on the other side. "Not yet," she whispered.

He slid his palm over the door as his shadows licked ineffectively against its painted wood, driven by undeniable longing. For a fleeting moment, he thought he felt her warmth through the barrier.

Even when he'd possessed his physical body, he'd never desired anyone as much as he desired Josephine Davis. His time with the queen—who'd been ethereal and impossibly beautiful —had been a dalliance, an exploration of curiosity. Despite her power, his lust for her had been minimal. Their coming together had primarily served to solidify a mutually beneficial arrangement. But Sophie's allure possessed a strength he could not ignore.

She wanted him, too, but resisted for reasons he couldn't fully understand. To be so close to her with that knowledge was torturous—more so than any curse the queen could have laid upon him.

He could not deny the truth; his want for Sophie now exceeded his desire to be free of his curse.

CHAPTER NINE

SOPHIE ADJUSTED her position for the umpteenth time; no matter how she lay, she couldn't get comfortable enough to fall asleep. The mattress was too lumpy, or too hard, or too soft, and her pillow felt either flat as a board or stuffed so full that it bent her neck to an extreme angle. When her arms weren't stiff and uncomfortable, her legs were restless. And she knew why.

She was aroused.

Her skin was hot and overly sensitive, her breasts full and weighty, her nipples tight and hard, and her sex was slick with need. She craved the cool, soothing caress of shadowy hands.

Flopping onto her back, she slapped her arms against her sides and glared up at the ceiling.

Who am I kidding? I'm not even tired.

After retreating from the porch, she'd eaten a quick dinner, showered, and put some water and food in the rabbit's box. She'd considered going to bed the safest, most logical step after that. She just had to close her eyes and forget all about what had transpired between her and Cruce. But from the moment she lay down, all she could do was imagine the feel of his shadows on her skin while his husky, guttural voice echoed through her mind.

Let me in.

It had been too soon. Telling him about Tyler, about the hell she'd lived through, had reminded her how fresh those wounds remained. They'd scabbed over, and she'd torn those scabs off to let them bleed all over again.

Despite that, she *wanted* to let Cruce in.

Why hadn't she?

I'm not...myself when I'm with him. I feel so much. *He tempts me, arouses me, consumes me. What if he seeks to control me, too?*

No. I'm in control of this. He gave me power over him.

But how much control did she really have? How absolute was it?

Oath or not, she believed that Cruce would never cause her harm, especially after seeing his reaction when he'd thought the blood on her shirt was hers. But the highest, most rational part of her mind said it was stupid to trust him. She should've known better by now. And yet...

Something within her, something deeper and more meaningful than both her conscious and subconscious mind, had recognized Cruce's presence as a comfort from the beginning. What he *was* had frightened her, what he could *do* remained unsettling, but she did not fear him. He was a balm to her battered soul.

She closed her eyes, attempting to ignore her body's demands, and strained for the peaceful oblivion of sleep. When she turned her mind toward mundane matters, her thoughts simply circled back to Cruce.

Groaning, Sophie kicked off the covers. Cool air settled over the bare skin of her legs. It wasn't enough—it would never be enough, because it wasn't *him*. She closed her eyes and finally relented to her desires.

She lifted her hands, settled them over her breasts, and

squeezed, brushing her fingers over her nipples through her nightshirt. The sensation was but a whisper, a poor substitute for what she truly craved. She needed more.

Biting her lip, Sophie eased the hem of her nightshirt up over her hips, flattened her palm on her stomach, and slid her hand beneath the waistband of her underwear. Her fingers delved into the wet heat of her sex. She pressed a fingertip to her clit and worked it in small, slow circles. Her breath hitched as her pleasure steadily built.

She quickened the pace.

Her orgasm was short and swift. She gasped, squeezed her eyes shut, and slammed her thighs closed against the sensation. Though her breath was ragged, she felt no more sated than before. If anything, her arousal had only increased; her sex throbbed, wet and...

Hollow.

The entire act seemed hollow, devoid of emotion, of meaning.

I can fulfill your desires.

Her eyes snapped open. Had she heard Cruce with her ears or in her head?

"Let me in, Sophie," he beckoned, his voice soft, alluring, and inhuman.

She looked at the window. A pair of faintly glowing eyes stared back at her from amidst a patch of darkness.

He'd watched her. She clenched her thighs around her hand. Rather than the embarrassment she would've expected, she found herself strangely excited. Her desire sparked anew. She lazily stroked her clit as she stared into his eyes; their glow intensified.

"Let me in, Josephine Davis."

His voice, though muted by the glass, swept through her. She was tempted, so tempted...

She panted as her thighs eased apart.

127

"Sophie…"

It's what I want.

She wasn't scared of him, only of what he made her feel. Sophie *wanted* him.

"Cruce," she rasped as she continued to stroke herself, "come to me."

He faded away, clearing the window space to allow silvery moonlight to stream through. She waited, holding her breath, yearning for his touch.

The darkness on the windowsill deepened gradually; she didn't realize it was in motion until it flowed down the wall, shifting like a shadow cast by a moving light source. The air seemed to cool further, raising anticipatory goosebumps on her skin.

Shadows coalesced at the foot of her bed to form a tall figure with huge antlers jutting off its head.

Cruce's starlight eyes fell upon her. "Remove your coverings, mortal."

Sophie's heart leapt. She'd been forced to follow commands for years, but this command…this one she *wanted*, and it made her burn with longing.

She slid her hand out from between her thighs and hooked the sides of her underwear with her fingers. Lifting her backside, she pulled her panties down her legs until she was able to kick them off. She grasped the hem of her nightgown next and drew it up, over her head, tossing it onto the floor.

She lay bare before the Lord of the Forest.

"Spread your legs, Josephine." Though his eyes didn't seem to move, she felt his gaze trail down her body like a physical touch.

With her hands curled into loose fists on either side of her head, Sophie slowly parted her thighs, exposing her sex.

Cruce's form swelled, billowing outward like spreading smoke. He flowed over the bed, tendrils of shadow creeping over the sheets ahead of his main mass to slide over her legs.

They felt like little puffs of cool air blown by a lover. As he neared, the tendrils twisted together to form arms. His hands glided along her outer thighs and the curves of her hips.

His antlered head dropped between her legs. Sophie's breath caught in her throat as she felt the chilled slide of his long, pliable tongue over her slick folds. He produced a low, ravenous hum that vibrated across her skin.

"Oh God," Sophie moaned, tilting her pelvis toward him.

"What do you ask of me, mortal?" he purred and licked her again. "What do you desire?"

His touch affected her deeply, seeming more substantial than ever before, but his voice was just as powerful. Delicious heat flared low in her belly.

"I want…" She bit her lip, cutting off a sharp moan as she arched her back.

"What do you *need*, Josephine?" His shadowy hands moved over her sides to cover her breasts, pearling her nipples with their chill.

His tongue swirled around her clit before slipping *inside* her, stroking her inner walls, as more hands settled over her bare skin. Cruce's darkness consumed her; it swallowed the bedroom, the moonlight, and drew Sophie into a world where only the two of them existed. The pleasure he inflicted upon her built and built until it burst in a wave of exquisite torment.

"You!" she cried out as she writhed upon the sheets. Her climax rippled through her, tensing her limbs and producing a gush of liquid heat between her thighs.

"*Yes*," Cruce growled, his shadowy form rising over her. He caged her in his arms. Misty wisps of darkness licked at her shoulders, but his body appeared more composed, more corporeal, than ever before.

Panting, she stared up into his blazing eyes.

"And you will have me, Sophie." He entered her sex. His cool, ghostlike touch flowed over her slick flesh, permeating her, stroking all the right places so lightly that it was maddening. Though her vaginal walls didn't stretch, he *filled* her. The part of him within Sophie moved ceaselessly, pulsing like an electric current to send thrills throughout her body.

She moaned and reached for him. Her hands encountered no physical form, but the space he occupied was thicker than air, denser, just how she'd imagined it would feel to touch a cloud when she was young. She moved beneath him, her skin thrumming with his supernatural ministrations. A tendril of shadow trailed over her breasts and down her middle, toward her pelvis. It delved between her thighs to stroke her clit.

"I *will* claim you, Josephine," Cruce rasped.

A stronger pulse flared within Sophie's sex and she gasped, squeezing her eyes shut as her head fell backward.

"I will feel your heat," Cruce continued. The vibrations within her quickened. "I will drink your sweet nectar." Another pulse, more intense than the last. Sophie cried out. "And I will taste your very essence."

He lowered his head, his eyes brighter than she'd ever seen. "Soon, you will be *mine*."

Immense pleasure blasted through Sophie, lighting up every nerve in her body. She screamed his name as she came, and he settled atop her, enveloping her, making it impossible to know where he ended and she began. He was in her, around her, part of her very being. She felt him *everywhere*.

When she finally came down from the heights of her passion, she could do little more than lay there, exhausted but sated, every inch of her skin tingling with the aftermath of Cruce's attention. Though the intensity of his touch diminished, he didn't withdraw from her. His nearness soothed her.

Soon, her eyelids grew heavy, and she sighed as weariness draped over her. "Cruce..."

"I am here, Sophie," he said gently, stroking her cheek.

Sophie closed her eyes and smiled. She felt him, inside and

out, and that didn't frighten her. Even when he'd blocked out all the light, she hadn't been afraid. With Cruce, she was...safe.

CRUCE RELISHED SOPHIE'S WARMTH. He possessed no willpower by which to draw away from her, no desire to deprive himself of the sensations she awoke within him—each of which was more intense than anything he'd ever felt. Even though the experience was incomplete, even though there was so much missing, it was overwhelming. What would it be like when he could truly touch her and taste her? When he could slide into her and feel her inner walls clutching his cock to draw him deeper?

His own contentment at that moment was driven by so much—her pleasure, her body's response to his attention, her scent, her heat. Her enjoyment and satisfaction were reward enough, but he'd received something else, too. Whether knowingly or not, she'd transferred fresh, potent life force to him while in the throes of passion. It had been more powerful than any he'd consumed during his curse.

He'd not drained her at all; though her essence was tantalizing, he felt no compulsion to feed from it, and he refused to harm her regardless. Her life force felt just as strong as it always had, if not more so, as though bolstered by her contentment. She'd given to him without taking from herself. It made no sense to Cruce, but he accepted it; he didn't need to understand every aspect of his irresistible attraction to Sophie to accept it.

She was made to be his, and he was meant to be hers.

The thought was jarring. One of the unspoken rules of his world had always been never to cede power without receiving something equal or greater in exchange. This was not a relationship between a fae queen and a forest lord, and there were no immense magical forces at work. He stood to gain nothing but some joy—fleeting joy, given her mortal lifespan—by offering himself to Josephine Davis. She could not protect him, she could not reinforce his realm in any meaningful fashion, and she possessed no magic by which to break his curse or battle potential enemies.

But he wanted to belong to her, all the same.

"Josephine…" he said softly, continuing to stroke her bare skin.

She stirred, stretching her limbs. "Hmm?"

He hesitated. How much did he *need* to tell her? Withholding information was not the same as lying, and she didn't need to know all his secrets. It would be foolish to instill so much trust in a human.

And yet he *wanted* to tell her. He wanted her to know that she had his trust no matter what was to come, no matter what choice she made.

"All Hallows Eve falls in three nights, and it will be lit by a full moon. From moonrise to sunrise, I will have physical form."

A crease appeared between her brows, and she opened her eyes. "You're talking about Halloween? What do you mean?"

"It is an aspect of my curse. On that night, the veil between the spirit realm and the physical realm is…thinned. When it coincides with the full moon, I am granted my body, my flesh and blood, until the next day dawns and the veil is restored."

She sat up and scooted back to lean against the iron head-board. Cruce flowed off her, remaining on the bed but severing the contact between them; she needed to know she was free of his influence in this, needed to know that she was making her own choice.

Her gaze moved over him, and Cruce studied her in turn. He took in her slender neck, her narrow shoulders, and her small, pert breasts. His eyes roved over her legs, which still glistened with evidence of her pleasure, and shifted toward the treasure between her thighs.

"You… Will you still be a shadow?" she asked.

"No. I will be as I once was...though I will possess none of my old power."

"So...I'll be able to actually touch you? And you...you'll be able to touch *me*?" Her cheeks flushed, but she didn't look away.

"Yes." He slid a tendril forward and brushed it over her ankle. The teasing bit of warmth that seeped into him was almost too much to bear. "On that night, I wish for nothing more than to join with you. Flesh to flesh."

He could hear her heart beating rapidly, but her expression conveyed anticipation rather than fear.

"I want that, too." She ran her fingers through the tendril on her ankle. "I feel you now. You're more...solid than before."

How would she handle the full truth of that? He didn't want to frighten her, didn't want to turn her away when she was finally accepting her desires. Learning that he'd killed four humans was not likely to keep her at ease...

"The closer we draw to All Hallows Eve, the more substantial I become. In the months before you arrived here, I was barely able to interact with the physical world."

She frowned. "So...what happens after Halloween? Will I be able to see you, to hear you?"

"For a time, yes. But eventually, I will only be able to interact with you after I feed."

"Feed? Is that... That's what you did to the bear, isn't it?"

Cruce withdrew from her once again, but he remained on the bed. It didn't seem right to maintain his touch as he spoke of such matters.

"It is. I tore the life force from its body and absorbed it into myself."

Her eyes flared, and her lips parted. "I...I thought that was what happened, but I didn't know for sure."

"It is another aspect of my curse. The queen knew I drew power from my forest—from its plants and animals, from its natural balance. The cycles of life and death, growth and decay, are essential, and they feed into one another. When balanced, I am at my peak power. Her curse makes me dependent upon the life force of other beings, makes me hunger for it until it drives me mad and I have no choice but to feed. It sustains me. And, in doing so, the balance is disrupted, weakening my forest—weakening me."

"Why haven't you fed from me?"

He swept his gaze over her again; he desired ever more of her, but his hunger hadn't pertained to her life force since shortly after he'd met her. "Because you are meant to be mine. Part of me recognized that even before I knew it was true."

Fear gleamed in her eyes; he recognized it as the same fear she'd harbored when speaking of Tyler. It was the fear that had driven her to this place to begin with. He extended a hand and settled it lightly over her foot.

"I do not seek to control you, Josephine Davis."

"What then? What do you want from me other than..." She motioned to her naked form.

"*Everything.*" He held her gaze, and to her credit, Sophie did not look away. "But there must be balance. If you are mine, then I am also yours...and I will give all of myself to you."

Her brows furrowed. "I...guess I still don't understand. I'm human, and you're...whatever you are. A spirit, a forest lord, a shadow." She shook her head. "And we *just* met." She paused, seemed to once more take note of her state of undress, and flushed.

When she reached for the blanket, he halted her with a gentle touch on her hand. "We just met, Josephine, and yet you *feel* the connection just as I do."

"I don't—"

"You *do.* I have seen it in your eyes. You struggle against it even now, because you fear losing what power you have regained, but I would never take that from you."

She pressed her lips together, jaw muscles ticking.

"You are my mate." He moved closer, trailing a shadowy hand along her jaw and slipping his fingers into her hair as he rose over her. "And I am yours. That is why I am so drawn to you, why I cannot stay away. Why I can do you no harm."

Sophie's breath quickened. She raised a hand and settled it over his. "There's no way to break your curse?"

"There *must* be, but it is outside my knowledge."

She dropped her gaze. Her expression was thoughtful, determined, and anguished all at once. When she looked back at him, there was resolve in her eyes. "Then we will give what we can to each other." She turned her face toward his hand as his shadows rippled over her. "And in three days, I will be yours completely, and you will be mine."

Cruce hummed low and slipped a tendril of shadow around one of her knees, parting it from the other. Her desirous scent strengthened. He would have given anything to be able to truly taste her.

He slid the tendril along her inner thighs and stroked the heat of her glistening sex. "I do not intend to ignore my hunger for you in the meantime, mortal."

A fiery thrill coursed through his being as Sophie laid back with a moan and opened to him again.

CHAPTER TEN

THE NEXT TWO days passed faster than Sophie had thought possible. The morning after that blissful night with Cruce, she'd woken to an orgasm with his name on her lips, her body quivering in overwhelming pleasure. It had all seemed like a dream in those first groggy moments, just like the others she'd experienced. But she turned to discover Cruce there with her. *He'd* brought her to climax, not a dream of him.

It was impossibly arousing and erotic to watch his shadowy form, made faint in the dim morning light, move over her body, to have his head between her thighs. She yearned to grasp his antlers and pull him closer, to grind her sex upon his mouth and tongue, to *feel* him inside and out.

The entire situation was shocking, strange, and exhilarating. She'd never taken charge in the bedroom before. Not long into her marriage to Tyler, she'd wanted *nothing* to do with sex, whether with him or anyone else. But with Cruce…

Despite her initial fear, Sophie had been drawn to Cruce from the start. She'd dreamed of him before she'd even known of his existence. And these last two days had been *wonderful*. He touched her often, and whenever they weren't in contact, she found herself craving his touch. She needed that connection with him, needed to know he was near.

Halloween couldn't come fast enough.

One more day. Just one more day.

Then she'd be able to see him, kiss him, and feel him. She was both excited and nervous. For the first time in so long, Sophie felt...cherished. Cared for. *Safe*. And she wanted their joining to reflect the growing feelings she held for him.

He'd told her more about his past, about the fae court he'd never wanted to be part of, and his forest. Every time he spoke of his domain, he spoke with pride, love, and sorrow. It pained him that he had to take from his land to survive, and no amount of research on Sophie's part had given her any leads to help him —there were hundreds of thousands of articles, blogs, and websites dedicated to occult topics that might have been relevant, but how much of it was *credible*? Everything she'd found on fairy curses was vague at best.

It was as he'd told her—humans had lost the bulk of whatever knowledge they may once have possessed regarding his world.

Sophie had just removed the pan of baked chicken from the oven when her laptop rang with an alert from Facetime. Her heart leapt. She quickly set the pan atop the stove, tossed her oven mitts down, and raced to the computer. She accepted the call.

"Kate!" Sophie grinned when her friend's face appeared on the screen. It'd been days since they last spoke. But her smile died when she noticed the distress on Kate's face.

"Oh my God, Sophie! Where've you been? I've been trying to get a hold of you for two days now!"

A pang of guilt pierced Sophie's chest. "I'm so sorry. I wasn't thinking, and I let the laptop battery die." She'd only realized it this afternoon and had plugged it in immediately. She hadn't even taken her phone out of her bag since the last time she was in town, so it was likely dead, too. "Is everything okay?"

Kate bit her lip, glanced at something off-camera, and shook her head. "No. I don't think so. I...I don't know. I'm just worried, and you have no idea how scared I was when I couldn't reach you. You're okay? Nothing strange going on? You're safe?"

Unease filled Sophie. "I'm fine. Why? What's wrong? You're scaring me, Kate."

"He was here, Sophie."

"*What*? But he didn't—"

"I know! But I think... Look, I'm not sure. I saw him talking to some of the neighbors yesterday, probably asking questions, and one of them might have seen us together and said something. He came here asking if I'd seen you. Said that you were missing, and he was worried. He was playing the concerned husband. When I told him I had no idea where you were, he insisted that someone saw you here, that I was your secret friend. I didn't give him anything, and he got really agitated. He insisted I was helping you, and I had to scare him off by threatening to call the cops."

Sophie dropped into her chair, heart pounding. She wrung her hands in her lap. "Did you? Call the cops?"

"No. He went home. But Sophie..." Kate leaned closer to the camera, eyes intent. "I went out to get my mail today. I hadn't checked it in a couple days and...your card was in there. The one you sent me for my birthday. It was torn open. I know you didn't put a return address, but it was postmarked in Raglan."

Dread churned in Sophie's stomach. She swallowed thickly to keep her lunch down.

"His car's still in the driveway," Kate continued, "but I haven't seen him for a while. I need you to be careful, okay? If you want me to come stay with you, I can leave tonight."

Sophie was silent, her breath rapid and shallow.

"Sophie?" Kate pressed.

139

Sophie shook her head. "No. No, it's okay. I'll be fine." The cabin was twenty minutes outside of town, and miles away from the main road. That was buffer enough, if he decided to make the hours-long drive to get here…wasn't it? Regardless, she had Cruce. He'd protect her.

"Okay…" Kate frowned. "But let me know if you change your mind, and I'll be on my way."

"I…I need to go," Sophie said, raising a shaky hand to disconnect the call. She couldn't have Kate coming here, couldn't have her involved any more than she already was. And Cruce was here…

Cruce.

"Sophie, wait. Are—"

"I-I'm fine. Goodnight," Sophie said quickly. She clicked the icon and disconnected the call.

She stared, unseeing, at the computer screen.

He knows. He knows I'm here. He'll find me.

She pressed a hand to her chest. Her heart fluttered against her palm, beating much too quickly.

"Cruce," she whispered. Her throat felt tight, and she struggled to take in air.

He'll hurt me. He'll make me pay.

Sophie got to her feet, took two steps, and collapsed as her knees gave out. She threw an arm out, slapping her palm flat on the floor to catch herself before she landed face-first, and clutched at her chest with her free hand.

He'll kill me. Oh God, he'll kill me.

She panted, gasping for air as hot tingles spread across her face. Darkness encroached on the edges of her vision. She tried to focus on the carpet fibers, tried to shrug off the dizziness, to cling to consciousness.

"No. I can't…can't. I need to…stay awake."

"Sophie?" Cruce's voice crashed over her, and the note of panic within it—something she'd never expected to hear from him—only heightened her anxiety.

"Can't...breathe," she rasped. "My heart..."

He settled over her, a cool presence, a suggestion of weight. Shadow darkened her vision further, but this wasn't tunnel vision. This was *Cruce*.

"It is racing," he said. His words surrounded her in a gentle, otherworldly whisper. "Tell me how to help you. How do I make you better?"

"Stay...with me and...talk."

His body moved around her, creating delicate trails of sensation on her skin. His touch was as ethereal as ever, but there was something more to it now—a promise.

A moment later, he gave voice to that promise. "Tomorrow night, beneath the silver light of the moon, I will soothe your skin with my own hands, Josephine Davis. I will show you pleasure like you have never known, I will worship you like you are my world, my lady, my goddess."

He pressed on her back; the increased pressure might have startled her at any other time, but as it spread over her, she found only comfort in it. He was real, and he was here. Her shadow. Her protector. Her mate.

"Breathe, Sophie. Smoothly, easily. Breathe for me, who has not lungs to draw in air. Breathe so that my first breath tomorrow night may be spent in kissing you."

Sophie closed her eyes and inhaled deeply, filling her lungs as much as she was able before slowly releasing the breath. She did it over and over, and it grew a little easier each time. Her heart ceased its rapid beating, and as her panic eased, exhaustion bore down upon her.

She sniffled, sinuses burning with the threat of tears. She opened her eyes. Her vision had cleared, but wisps of shadow roiled around her, made hazy by the interior lights.

"I'm okay," she said softly. "I'm okay now."

He withdrew from her and formed himself into a more

substantial shadow immediately in front of Sophie. Despite the illumination from overhead, his eyes were bright as they settled upon her.

"What happened, Sophie? What was this? Your life force was undiminished, but I could taste your fear in the air."

"A panic attack," she replied, easing herself down into a sitting position and leaning back against the wall. She settled a hand over her heart. It still beat faster than normal, but at least it was steady. "I never used to have them until…"

"Until *him*," Cruce growled.

"Yes."

"What caused this?"

"I talked to Kate. I think he knows I'm here. Well, not *here*, but in the area." Just thinking about Tyler and imagining what he'd do if he found her had Sophie's heart picking up speed again. "He's looking for me."

Cruce extended a hand, brushing his cold fingers over her cheek. "And should he come here in search of you, I will ensure he never looks anywhere again."

Sophie leaned into his misty touch and closed her eyes. Tomorrow. Tomorrow she would actually *feel* Cruce.

"You are safe here, Sophie. Safe with me."

"Hold me?" she asked. "I need to feel you right now."

He silently glided forward and enveloped her, blanketing her in darkness and cold that had become too familiar to be anything but soothing to her now. His soft touch trailed over her body in a dozen places, chasing away her lingering tension.

"Thank you," Sophie said, closing her eyes. Her confidence and courage wouldn't return overnight, but she knew, in time, they'd come back. For now, she had Cruce to ease her, to calm her, to be her strength when she was weak.

"You are mine, Josephine Davis," Cruce whispered into her ear. "*Nothing* will take you from me."

CHAPTER ELEVEN

ANTICIPATION THRUMMED in Sophie's belly as she drove along forested roads. She had shopping to do.

Tonight.

The word repeated over and over in Sophie's head like a mantra. She couldn't remember ever feeling so light, so giddy with excitement, so...*happy*. She felt like a bride on the morning of the dream wedding she'd been waiting for all her life.

And she wanted tonight to be perfect.

Now that she looked back on it, she realized that she'd never felt this sort of elation when she married Tyler. It was more proof that in some deep, instinctual part of her mind, she'd known. She'd known what kind of man he was. Had known that he...wasn't Cruce.

For a long time, Sophie had thought something was wrong with her. Sex had been mediocre—she'd rarely orgasmed during the act, and kissing had always seemed sloppy and unappealing. She knew now that sex with Tyler had always been a matter of him taking and never giving. It was nothing like the passion lovers shared in books and movies; fictional romance was always looked down upon as unrealistic, but was it truly so unrealistic for a woman to want the man she loved to give as much to her as she did to him?

But she hadn't been in love with Tyler. She'd just been naïve, had allowed herself to get caught up in his charm…

Sophie shook her head, shoving those thoughts away.

Not today. Today, she wouldn't think about Tyler. She refused to let him ruin any more of her life.

She followed the highway through town; she doubted the few stores in Raglan carried what she intended to buy. Kids were already out in their costumes, trick-or-treating at the small businesses along the main road. Sophie smiled at the joy on their faces. It was Saturday—the best day of the week for Halloween—and the town was busier than she'd ever seen.

Sophie continued for another thirty minutes to her destination, Silverglade, which was popular in the region due to its large mall. The mall parking lot was packed, and it took a good ten minutes to find a parking spot that wasn't a mile away from an entrance.

Once inside, the aromas of brewing coffee, pumpkin spice, and cinnamon struck her in full force, and she inhaled them deeply. Sophie loved this time of year.

The shops were filled with people; just like in Raglan, there were costumed children everywhere, and many of the stores had employees standing out front with bowls of candy to pass out. In the center of the mall there was a photobooth, a face-painting station, and several games set up for the kids. Black and orange posters announced a costume contest that afternoon.

It'd been a long time since Sophie was around so many people. At first, it induced a sense of claustrophobia, and she feared an impending attack. But the laughter, smiles, and relaxed attitude soon eased her anxiety. Everyone was having fun, and she didn't have bruises, black eyes, or split lips to worry about someone noticing. She was free from that.

She went into several stores in her search for the perfect thing to wear for Cruce. She discovered it in the last apparel shop she visited. It was a long, black satin nightgown with two thin straps and a bodice trimmed with lace leaves that was sure to show off some cleavage. The color reminded her of Cruce.

Sophie smirked. It was Halloween; what better a costume for her gothic wedding night?

She purchased some make up from another shop and couldn't resist her first pumpkin spice latte of the season as she left.

Her excitement only grew on the drive home. A new idea occurred to her when she reached Raglan; she could make dinner for Cruce. He'd be mortal tonight. That meant he could eat, right?

Sophie blushed. If he had half the stamina in his physical form that he did as a shade, there wouldn't be any time to eat.

She stopped at the grocery store and ran inside, picking up a few things to throw together just in case. She pulled her cart into Doris's lane and piled her items on the belt.

"You look like you have something exciting planned tonight," Doris said with a cheeky smile.

Sophie returned the smile. "I do."

Doris gave her the eye. "A man, I take it?"

Not exactly...

Sophie chuckled at her own thought and nodded. "Yeah. Kind of...our first date."

Doris bagged Sophie's groceries and rang up the total. "Pretty girl like you? I'm surprised you're not already snatched up."

Sophie's smile faltered. She pulled out a couple twenties and handed them to Doris. "Not very lucky, I guess."

Doris winked as she gave Sophie her change. "Let's hope you get lucky tonight."

Cheeks burning, Sophie laughed. "I think I will."

As she stepped outside, the hairs on the back of her neck rose, and a shudder traveled down her spine. The sensation was similar to what she'd felt on her first day at the cabin, but this time it seemed...*wrong*. She caught movement out of the corner of her eye and turned her head to scan the nearby pallets of wood pellets and ice melt. There was no one there.

Sophie dug out her phone as she walked to her car and dialed Kate.

"Hey! Are you in town?" Kate asked after accepting the call. "Everything okay?"

"Yeah, I'm fine, Kate. I just wanted to check in real quick." She switched the phone to her other hand as she checked the back seat of her car, opened the driver's door, and slid inside. "Is he still there?"

There was a several second delay. "His car is still there. I haven't seen him leave for a while."

Sophie released a long, relieved breath. "Thank you."

"Always."

Sophie switched to speaker phone and set down her cell. "So, you're going out for the first time with Steve tonight, right?" she asked as she started the car, backed out of her parking spot, and shifted into drive.

"Well...not the *first* time."

"You already went out with him!"

"Yes! Work's been really hectic this week—we have a client who *really* screwed up their bookkeeping—and I've been putting in extra hours. So, Steve took me out to try to give me a chance to unwind a little. That's part of why I missed your calls the other day..." Kate sighed heavily. "And then I got onto you for not answering. God, I'm such a shitty friend."

"No! Kate, no. You're wonderful," Sophie said as she turned

onto the highway. "I wouldn't even be here right now if it weren't for you. You can't feel responsible for me like that. You have your own life to live."

"But Tyler—"

"You can't put your life on hold for me, Kate. I'll be fine. I… met someone, too."

"What? Really? Who? Why am I just now hearing about this?"

"It's…still too new. I don't want to say too much until I know for sure." But Sophie knew already—Cruce was hers. There was just no way she could explain to Kate who and what Cruce was. Hell, she couldn't even give Kate his name. "Tell me more about Steve."

"Oh, Sophie, I think he's the one! He is the kindest, sweetest, most considerate man I've ever met. It doesn't hurt that he's *packing*, if you know what I mean."

Sophie gasped. "Did you?"

"*Best* sex of my life!"

Sophie laughed.

"And his kids?" Kate continued. "They're adorable!"

They talked for a little longer until the connection got staticky. Sophie said a quick goodbye just before the signal dropped completely.

Once she made it home, she collected her purchases and went inside. Cruce wouldn't come until that night; he'd told her the daytime leading up to the full moon was particularly draining to him, and he needed time to prepare himself. She guessed it was a delicate way of saying that he needed to spend his time feeding to gather his strength.

Sophie prepped the food and stored it in the fridge; it would be ready toss in the oven if the opportunity arose.

She took a long, luxuriating shower before carefully applying her makeup. She kept it light and natural, just enough to make her eyes stand out, and after a bit of indecision, decided to keep her hair loose and flowing.

Stepping out of the bathroom in a towel, Sophie entered her room and lifted the nightgown off the bed. In hindsight, it wasn't the most practical thing to wear on a cool autumn night, but no matter what she wore, she doubted it'd be on for long.

And she'd have Cruce to keep her warm.

Sophie bit her lip and squeezed her thighs together. Just the thought of feeling his warm, strong touch made her sex pulse in need.

Soon.

Removing the tag from the garment, Sophie pulled it over her head. The fabric whispered over her skin like a silken caress. She turned to her dresser mirror. Her pale skin stood out against the black material, especially in the deep-cut *V* bustline. She spun, laughing, and joy shone bright in her dark eyes as she met her own gaze in the mirror. When was the last time she'd felt *beautiful*?

"Cruce," she said, thrilling in the feel of his name on her lips. Her lover.

Now, all she had to do was wait.

MINUTES FELT LIKE HOURS, and hours felt like days. She'd passed the time pacing and glancing out the window over and over, taking several brief breaks to check her makeup and hair. The wait was excruciating; all she wanted was for the damned sun to fall, even though she knew it was just one part of the equation.

She'd checked the charts—moonrise was twenty minutes after sunset.

Her anticipation reached a new peak when the final rays of sunlight finally left the evening sky, dropping the forest outside into gloomy twilight. She turned off the inside lights so she could see through the windows and continued pacing, eyes darting frequently to the clock. What if the charts were wrong? What if this didn't work out how they wanted it to?

Sophie shook off her doubts. When the clock said it was five minutes until moonrise, she couldn't help herself—she rushed outside and hurried off the porch, ignoring the chill in the air as she dashed barefoot across the driveway, over vegetation and fallen leaves, toward the forest. Heart pounding, she stopped before crossing the tree line and searched the shadows for Cruce.

Only her frantic heartbeat marked the passage of time. The leaves overhead sighed in a crisp breeze that chilled her exposed skin, but inside she was already ablaze. Gradually, silver light touched the violet sky between the branches, and she caught her first glimpse of the round, bright moon between the boughs of two trees.

She dropped her gaze and scanned the woods. Every shadow bristled with possibility, every hint of movement bore unspoken promise, every shaft of soft light could've been the one in which he would appear.

A snapping branch startled Sophie. She swung her gaze toward the sound to find herself looking down the old path, the same one she'd followed on the night Cruce had made himself known to her. Perhaps a hundred feet away, a large shadow loomed in the center of the path. As it approached her, its details grew clear—a humanoid shape with huge antlers and wide shoulders.

The volume of her heart beat increased, filling her ears, drowning out all other sounds.

The advancing shadow passed into a patch of silver light, and Sophie's breath hitched. It was her first glimpse of Cruce as he had been, as he was always meant to be.

His long, many-pointed antlers swept up and backward from pale, shimmering hair that hung around his broad shoulders. His eyes gleamed silver with reflected light, set in a face that was at once elfin, masculine, and bestial. Strands of his hair were tucked behind pointed ears that reminded her of a deer's. Her eyes lingered on his full lips, which promised wicked delights, before dipping lower.

Cruce's torso was powerful, sculpted muscle, the ridges and contours accentuated by the deep shadows cast by the moonlight. His expansive shoulders and chest tapered down to a narrow waist, where the muscles of his abs dipped toward his pelvis in an enticing, arousing *V*. His thick, strong arms swung casually at his sides, ending in large hands with claw-tipped fingers. Shaggy white fur began just above his hips, continuing down his long legs, from between which jutted his partially erect cock.

Sophie released a slow exhalation; his long, thick shaft ended in a bulbous head. She squeezed her thighs together against a sudden surge of lust.

As he lifted his leg in his graceful stride, she could not ignore the cloven hoof at its end.

Sophie drew her eyes back up to meet his. He had to be nearly seven feet tall, even taller if she counted his antlers.

"Cruce," she whispered.

His footfalls were startlingly quiet as he closed the remaining distance between them. For an instant, she was aware of the immense heat radiating from him, and then he swept her into his arms, lifted her off her feet, and pressed his lips to hers.

Sophie gasped, and he took advantage of her parted lips to deepen the kiss. His tongue slipped into her mouth to explore its depths, to taste her, and she responded in kind. She raised her arms and looped them around his neck. His warmth flowed into her; his hands were like branding irons, running over her back, shoulders, and ass, drawing her ever closer.

Her desire was a blazing inferno, blistering hot. When she moaned against his lips, Cruce growled, and the sound vibrated to her core. Overwhelming need, unlike anything she'd ever felt, tore through her, clouding her mind to everything but Cruce.

Her mate.

Her dark lover.

CHAPTER TWELVE

CRUCE CLUTCHED SOPHIE'S WARM, soft body against him, unable to keep his hands from roaming over her. Though he'd never known it, *this* was the moment he'd awaited since before he was ever cursed, since before he'd ever met the fae queen, since the day he'd come into existence. Josephine Davis had always been the thing he was meant to desire above all else. She was woven into his being, she was the thread that completed the tapestry of his fate. She was *his*.

Her shimmering gown looked lovely, but it was an unacceptable barrier between Cruce and her bare flesh. His need to touch her, to feel and taste her, had grown immensely in the days he'd known her, and he could not deny himself now. He had one night with her, one night to imprint himself upon her soul and emblazon her forever into his memory. There was no way to know if she'd be here the next time his curse allowed him physical form; human lives were so fleeting, so delicate…

Were he not trapped in this mortal form, separated from his magic, he'd have granted her a portion of his life force just to ensure she'd be awaiting him when next the full moon rose on All Hallows Eve.

But this was the time for reflection. He would spend this night enjoying every moment they could share to the fullest. This sample of her was sublime, but he craved a more complete taste.

Inhaling deeply her sweet, satisfying scent, Cruce knelt on the forest floor. He leaned forward and laid Sophie on a bed of fallen leaves, guiding her arms away from his neck. Without hesitation, he grasped the material of her gown and tore it apart down the middle, exposing her pale skin to the night air.

Sophie gasped, kiss-swollen lips parting as her eyes flared. His gaze trailed down the length of her body. Her breasts, tipped with hard, pink nipples, rose and fell with quick breaths. He'd taste those soon enough, but first, he needed a *deeper* taste...

The final barrier between them was an arousing scrap of black lace covering her sex. Cruce lowered his head and breathed in the fragrance of her desire, which was undiminished by the material. It filled his senses, mixing with her lavender and vanilla aroma. Her scent was a hundred times stronger than it had been in his shade form. He stiffened, his muscles tensing, and his lips drew back, bearing his fangs in a snarl. His cock extended fully from its sheath, granite hard and throbbing, aching to be buried deep in Sophie's little body, to feel her heat clench tight around it.

"Ah, Sophie. My Josephine..."

The female laid out before him, his *mate*, was primed and ready. His every instinct was to turn her onto her hands and knees, mount her, and wildly rut until they were both too exhausted to move—and then take her again.

Hooking the lacy fabric at each of her hips, he tore it apart, tossing the pieces aside, and spread Sophie's legs wide. His eyes fell upon her exposed sex. She was pink and petite, her delicate folds glistening with arousal.

Cruce dropped his head and buried his face between her

thighs, running the length of his long tongue from the bottom to the top of her sex, flicking her clit. She bucked her hips and released a cry. Her sweetness filled his mouth, ambrosial and heady, a natural aphrodisiac that made his cock ache for her all the more.

"Cruce!" Her voice was music in the twilight, and she followed his name with a series of breathy moans as she writhed atop the leaves.

He curled his arms beneath her legs and gripped her hips, pulling her closer and holding her in place, allowing no escape as he ravaged her with his tongue. He nipped her folds, explored her depths, and learned what his lovely mate enjoyed most by the motions of her body and the sounds escaping her lips.

Finally, Cruce latched onto her clit and sucked. She screamed and grasped his antlers with both hands. He growled against her, unrelenting, as she ground herself against his mouth in abandon. Sophie's scent strengthened as fresh nectar flowed from her. He released her clit and lowered his tongue, lapping at her sex before delving inside. Her inner walls fluttered, forcing another gush of nectar directly into his mouth. He drank it greedily.

Cruce did not still his tongue until most of the tension had fled her body and her cries had diminished into gentle moans. He pulled his face back to lick the moisture from her legs. Faint tremors coursed through her. Sophie's every reaction was a thrill to him; she'd released her inhibitions and offered herself to him without hesitation, without doubt, and for that she deserved everything he could give to her in return.

He eased her legs to either side of him and flattened a hand on her stomach.

How would she look with her belly rounded, carrying his offspring?

The thought sparked a need in him far more primal and

instinctual than any he'd experienced up to that moment; he would do all he could to ensure his seed took root.

He dropped a hand to the ground beside her head and met her gaze. Her eyes, half-lidded and dark with desire, stared up at him. She raised her arms, trailing her fingertips over his face. She touched his lips, his nose, his brow, and his ears, until she finally delved her fingers into his hair and pulled him down into a kiss. He groaned and returned the kiss, coaxing her tongue into a brief dance with his.

Tearing his mouth from hers, Cruce repositioned his hips and took his cock in hand. It pulsed with excruciating need. He pressed the head of his shaft to her center and thrust. Her gasp was sharp and sweet, as was the pain in his scalp as she tugged his hair.

"Sophie," he grated. He pulled his hips back and pushed again and again, easing himself deeper into her with every pump, urged on by her breathy moans and the sound of his name from her lips. Blissful heat enwrapped him.

Cold and darkness had built within him during his curse; though the years had been relatively few compared to his long existence, their toll had been immense. He'd not known the touch of a lover in almost two centuries. He'd not known true warmth in all that time. He could not fight his needs. Perhaps with anyone else, but not with his Josephine. And now that he had her he could not hold himself back.

Snarling, he braced his hands on the ground to either side of her, withdrew, and slammed back into her body. He didn't stop, didn't pause, didn't falter; he increased his speed, surging into and out of her again and again.

Sophie clung to him, her blunt nails biting into his arms as a series of sharp cries escaped her. His claws dug grooves in the dirt, and he growled, needing a deeper connection, needing more of her.

Gathering her in his arms, he sat back without pulling out of her body and positioned her to straddle his lap. Her dark, sultry eyes met his, and everything fell into place. She was *his*. Body and soul.

Settling his hands on her hips, he lifted and lowered her over his cock, thrusting his pelvis to meet her with increasing force. Her lashes fluttered, and she tilted her head back.

"Look at me, Josephine," Cruce commanded, baring his teeth as pleasure rippled through him.

Sophie raised her head and met his eyes again.

"You are *mine*," Cruce said, slamming her down harder, sinking deeper into her heat. "Mine. My mate. Say it!"

"Yours," she rasped through ragged breaths. She clenched his arms, and her sex tightened around his shaft. "Oh God, I'm going to—Cruce!"

He watched her face as she reached her peak, watched as bliss overcame her features. She trembled in his arms, her inner walls quivering and tugging his cock farther into her body. Heat poured from her and ran over his thighs, her heightened scent reminding him of the delicious flavor still lingering on his tongue; he'd taste it again before the night was through.

Immense pressure built within him, too powerful to contain. Now that he had her, the sensations were too much.

He would never get enough.

A maelstrom of pleasure ripped through him, tensing all his muscles at once. Her body had given freely of her life force when they'd come together before; this time, it demanded something of *him*, and he relented to its demands with a roar. His hips bucked as his cock pumped streams of hot seed into her.

Sophie cried out, scraping her nails over his back. Her body shuddered with another climax, drawing out more of his essence. Cruce's skin crackled with electric thrills; her sounds and reactions pushed his need ever higher, made him crave ever more of her. He was not yet satisfied. He had to claim her, to make her his fully.

Cruce pushed her back down onto the ground and swiftly followed, never breaking their connection. He braced himself over Sophie and drove his cock into and out of her, setting a wild, frantic pace. The sensation was so powerful it hurt. His harsh, guttural grunts mingled with her high-pitched moans to punctuate each thrust.

She threw her hands up to his chest and raked his skin, leaving delightful trails of fire in the wake of her fingertips. She arched and writhed beneath him, matching his frenzy, as feral as any of the creatures of his forest.

Their pleasure combined into something overwhelming. It stole Cruce's breath and made him curl his claws into the ground as it flowed through his veins to suffuse every fiber of his being. He panted through bared teeth, each inhalation drawing her scent in anew, ensuring that all his senses were awash with her.

When Sophie came, she screamed his name into the night. Cruce followed; as his seed exploded inside her again, he threw his head back and roared the name of her heart, of *his* heart —*Sophie*—proclaiming to his forest that the lord had found his lady. That he had given himself to her as much as he'd claimed her as his own. That despite his curse, he'd taken what was rightfully his.

He growled softly as they came down from the heights of their joining, the tiny, involuntary movements of their hips sparking fresh pulses of pleasure and coaxing everything from him a little at a time. Finally, the blinding haze of desire faded enough for Cruce to regain control of himself. He brushed locks of her auburn hair from her face and looked into her eyes, admiring their gentle glimmer in the silvery moonlight.

In all his existence, he'd never seen anything as beautiful as his Sophie was at that moment, aglow in the aftermath of their lovemaking. He settled a hand over her heart. Her tender, still-healing, mortal heart. It beat strongly beneath his palm.

"Cruce," Sophie whispered reverently.

"Josephine," he whispered back possessively.

She smiled at him, reaching up to place a hand on his chest. Her eyes shone with a reflection of everything he felt within himself—the unspoken emotions, the depth of their connection, the feeling that this moment, this joining, had been fated since the beginning of time. Whatever had drawn them together was unimportant, though; they had each other now, and that was the only thing that mattered.

"What the fuck?" said a male voice from behind Cruce.

Sophie stiffened, sucking in a sharp breath. The light in her eyes dimmed and took on a terrified cast.

That was sign enough for Cruce to know who had just arrived.

Snarling, Cruce withdrew from her, leapt to his feet, and spun to face the human.

The man—Tyler—staggered backward, eyes wide. He dipped a hand into his pocket and withdrew a dark object. A gun. He pointed the barrel toward Cruce.

Immediate, all-encompassing fury roiled within Cruce. This was the human who'd done so much harm to Sophie. The human who had scarred her physically and emotionally. The man who'd nearly killed her. And now he was here, on this night—the one night that Cruce had with her, when she'd finally overcome what Tyler had done to her and begun living again—with a weapon.

Sophie stood up behind Cruce, and he extended an arm to keep her there, staring at Tyler with teeth bared and brows low. At any other time, dispatching Tyler would've been simple. But this was the night that Cruce was mortal. It was the queen's cruel little tease—a night every twenty-or-so years during which Cruce could end his suffering, knowing that when the sun rose, he'd revert to his shade form and be doomed to two more decades of his curse with no escape.

Tyler's eyes flicked to the side, and Cruce knew he'd seen Sophie. She was pressed against Cruce, shaking in terror, her warm, rapid breaths flowing against his bare flesh.

"I come to bring you home and find you fucking some...*creature?*" Tyler spat in disgust. When Sophie didn't respond, he growled. "*Answer me, Josie!*"

"She does not answer to you," Cruce growled back, stepping toward the man.

"Stay the fuck back," Tyler warned, raising the gun higher.

"You are not welcome here, mortal. *Leave.*"

Tyler scowled, his thick brows furrowing. "You think you can tell me what to do?" His lips twitched and pressed into a tight line just before he changed the angle of the gun and fired it. Sophie screamed.

Cruce staggered back slightly as pain unlike he'd ever known exploded in his thigh.

"Cruce," Sophie breathed, placing her hands on his sides as though to steady him.

"Back the fuck up, Josie. Get away from that thing. *Now,*" Tyler said.

"No!" she cried; Cruce heard tears in her voice.

"No? Did you just tell me *no*?" Tyler kept the gun trained on Cruce, though he did not meet the forest lord's eyes. "If you don't move away from that thing right now, Josie, I'll shoot it again."

Cruce bared his fangs at Tyler. Fire blazed from the wound on his leg, but it only served to fuel his rage. The twenty feet of distance separating him from the man didn't feel like much—he could close it quickly—but the gun complicated matters. If Sophie was hit...

"She does not answer to you," Cruce repeated.

"Oh, she'll answer to me. She'll answer for every goddamned

thing she put me through. Do you hear me, Josie? As soon as I get my hands on you—"

"You will not touch her!" Cruce snarled.

The gun went off again, sending a projectile into Cruce's other leg. He grunted, and for an instant it seemed his knee was ready to buckle, but he would *not* fall to this human. Only one mortal could bring Cruce to his knees.

"No!" Sophie yelled, darting out from behind Cruce before his pain-delayed reaction could stop her. She positioned herself in front of him, arms splayed wide, her naked body a shield. "Don't. Please stop, Tyler. Don't do this."

Cruce's heart quickened, and his breath grew shallow. Even in this vulnerable form, his constitution was much greater than that of a human; if the bullets had been so damaging to him, what would they do to her? Ice pierced his chest and crept through his veins, colder than he'd ever felt even as a shade.

He'd only experienced this feeling once before, and then it had been fleeting and miniscule compared to what it was now.

Fear.

"You're seriously going to stand there, bare-ass naked with his cum dripping from your cunt, and tell me to stop?" Tyler's eyes narrowed on Sophie. "You're *my wife. Mine!*"

Cruce reached forward and placed a hand on Sophie's shoulder, meaning to guide her behind him again, but her feet were planted firmly. Despite his lack of magic, he understood somehow that it was more her willpower than her physical strength holding her in place. He admired her for it as much as he cursed her foolishness.

"I'm not your wife," Sophie said. "Not anymore. I'm his mate."

"Mate," Tyler echoed. He clenched his jaw and titled his head to one side, cracking his neck. "Come here, Josie."

"*Sophie,*" Cruce said in a low, warning tone. The man standing before them was worse than the hunters who'd so cruelly killed so many birds; Tyler had taken the concept of love and twisted it into *this*.

"No. I'm not leaving him."

"Come *here*," Tyler repeated, "or I'll blow its fucking brains out."

Sophie's body trembled under Cruce's palm, but she kept her back straight and shook her head. "No."

Why wouldn't she just *move*? Why wouldn't she keep herself safe?

Tyler's face contorted, shifting through a series of convoluted, frustrated emotions. His nostrils flared, the cords of his neck bulged, and he tilted his head in the other direction. "Fine," he finally said, aiming his gun at Sophie. "If you want to be a whore, you can die like one."

The cold in Cruce's blood suddenly expanded; it felt like countless needles stabbing him from within throughout his entire body. His oath was about to be broken. He'd sworn to protect her in his forest, to keep her safe, and the first true threat to have arisen since he gave her that word was going to be her end. And it was happening on the one night during which Cruce was vulnerable, the one night he was wholly disconnected from the senses that linked him to his forest.

The first night he was able to truly touch Sophie was also the night he was going to lose her.

Millennia of immortality blasted through his consciousness in a fraction of a second, filled with beauty and wonder, with contentment and sorrow, with the serenity and chaos of his domain. All of it paled in comparison to the ten days that had passed since he'd first seen Josephine Davis.

Grimacing, Tyler squeezed the trigger.

Cruce didn't hear the boom; he moved without further thought, lunging forward and shoving Sophie aside to assert himself between her and Tyler.

Something heavy punched into his chest, halting his

momentum. Tyler cursed and fired twice more, producing new points of impact across Cruce's ribcage.

Cruce glanced down. Dark crimson flowed from three holes in his chest, one of which was directly over his heart.

Despite his determination, his rage, his willpower, his legs refused to support his weight. His torso twisted as he fell, granting him full view of Sophie's pale, anguished face. When she screamed his name, her voice sounded far-away.

CHAPTER THIRTEEN

SOPHIE CRAWLED toward Cruce's fallen body. She ran her frantic hands over his face, repeating his name over and over, begging him to respond, *commanding* him to talk, to say something, *anything*. Tears streamed down her cheeks as she looked into his sightless eyes.

"No!" she wailed, pressing her forehead against his, shoulders quaking with her heart-wrenching sobs. "No, no, no, no. Cruce!"

She was oblivious to the blood, to the cold, to everything save her mate and the fading heat of the body he'd possessed for so short a time. Pain suffused her as her heart shattered. They hadn't even had a full night together.

A different kind of pain flared on her scalp as Tyler grasped a fistful of her hair. She screamed and fought the pull, clutching desperately at Cruce; she couldn't leave him, couldn't let him go.

Tyler wrenched her head back, tugging her away from her mate.

Sophie grasped his wrist and battled his hold, seeking a way to escape him, to relieve the pain as he dragged her across the ground.

"Let me go, you son of a bitch!" she yelled, kicking her legs and digging her heels into the earth beneath her. Twigs and rocks scraped her bare flesh. The world around her darkened as they crossed into the shadows under the canopy, leaving the moonlight behind.

"Got quite a mouth on you since you left, Josie."

"You killed him!" She slapped his arm.

Tyler ignored the blow, maintaining his pace. "Would have killed you, too, if it hadn't pushed you. You made me *that* mad, Josie! You cheated on me with that...thing! Do you know how much it hurt to see that? To find *my wife* getting fucked in the dirt by some...animal?" He growled and tightened his fingers, sharpening the pain on her scalp. "Guess you have another chance to learn your lesson now. You can still get put back in your place. You seem to have forgotten who you *really* belong to. But I'll show you. I'll make you remember that I'm it for you."

Gritting her teeth, Sophie reached higher and sunk her nails into his forearm, raking them downward as hard as she could.

"Fuck!" He released her and jerked his arm away with a hiss.

Sophie wasted no time; she scrambled to her feet and dashed away, ignoring the debris stabbing the soles of her feet. Her arms pumped at her sides and her breath sawed in and out of her lungs as she wove between the shadowed tree trunks. She just had to get back to the cabin.

Then she could even the odds.

A great weight slammed into her back and knocked her off her feet. She cried out before crashing to the forest floor face first, the air exploding from her lungs as something heavy fell atop her. Terror wrapped icy fingers around her heart.

Breath ragged, Tyler chuckled. "Do you really think you can run from me, Josie?"

He slid a hand around her, grasped her throat just under her jaw, and forced her head back. Sophie whimpered, squeezing her eyes shut.

"I'll always find you and bring you home," he rasped. The sour smell of alcohol washed over her. "Back to *me*. You know, you were easy to find once I knew where to look. Small town folk talk. I just needed to tell that nice old lady you were my wife, that I was back from the reserves and I couldn't get hold of you, and she gave me directions to your house." He pressed his face into her hair, inhaled, and groaned. "Do you know how much I missed you?"

Revulsion filled Sophie as he slipped his free hand under her to cup her breast and grinded his pelvis against her backside. She could feel his erection through his jeans.

He kissed her hair. "I might forgive you. Eventually. You'll have to prove yourself to me, of course, and beg for forgiveness." Withdrawing his arms, he pulled away from her for a moment before pressing a hand to her back, pinning her to the ground. He kicked her legs apart as something jingled.

He was unbuckling his belt.

"But right now, I need you, Josie. I need to...to undo this *taint*." Tyler moved his hands to her hips.

Panic seized Sophie.

"No!" She kicked at him and clawed the dirt, struggling to drag herself away.

Her foot connected with yielding flesh, and Tyler grunted. She gained a few precious feet, but it wasn't enough. He clamped his hand around one of her ankles in a viselike grip and dragged her back to him. She screamed, digging her fingers into the ground, but her strength couldn't match his.

He flipped her onto her back and fell upon her, wedging his hips between her thighs. Sophie didn't cease her struggles; she slapped and clawed at him, screaming all the while, though she knew there were no neighbors to hear her. She poured all her fear, pain, and hatred into her effort. She would not—could not —allow Tyler to do this. She couldn't let him try to erase the last memory she had of Cruce.

She belonged to the Lord of the Forest, and she'd die before allowing Tyler to sully her again.

"Enough!" Tyler yelled into her face, capturing her flailing arms. He transferred them to one of his rough hands and pinned them to the ground. He swung his other arm downward, slapping her across the face. Her vision blurred as stinging pain exploded from her jaw to her temple, silencing her cries.

As he drew back to hit her again, a blood-curdling roar echoed through the forest, unlike anything she'd ever heard from man or beast. It was filled with pain, anguish, and rage. It sounded from everywhere and nowhere at all.

Somehow, Sophie knew what that sound was.

Tyler hesitated, tearing his gaze away from Sophie to scan the surrounding woods, face paling. "What the fuck was that?"

His distraction was enough to allow her to pull her hands free. She thrust her palms against his chest and shoved, but he barely budged. She didn't allow that to deter her; after drawing in a deep breath, she screamed as loud as she could.

"Cru—"

Tyler clamped his fingers around her throat, cutting off her call, and turned his attention back to her with a glare. "Not. A. fucking. Sound."

A chill wind swept through the forest. Trees groaned, leaves rustled, and branches snapped. Tyler lifted his gaze again, eyes going wide. Keeping one hand on her throat, he reached around his back and drew his gun, leveling it at something outside Sophie's view. He fired once, twice, and then released her to take the gun in both hands and stand up.

She twisted away, swinging her attention in the direction he'd fired. A large, dark shape was slowly advancing toward them, a shadow with long antlers and wisps of darkness flowing from it like a tattered cloak. Tyler fired several more shots at the figure until the gun clicked, dry-firing.

"Shit," he spat.

The shadowy figure swayed to the side, disappearing into a tree.

Sophie turned to Tyler. He was fumbling with shaky hands to change the magazine in his gun. When the spare magazine slipped from his grasp, he bent forward, darting his hand out to catch it. Sophie didn't waste a moment; she kicked his hand as hard as she could, knocking the firearm from his grasp.

"Goddamned bitch!" He fell upon her again and drew back his fist. Sophie tensed, raising her arm and bracing herself for the blow.

Something thin and dark coiled around Tyler's wrist, halting his arm. For an instant, she thought it was shadow—Cruce's shadow—until she noticed the little leaves along its length.

Vines?

More vines lashed out, catching Tyler's other arm as he fought to free himself. He shouted, his voice growing desperate.

A vine crept over Sophie's leg. She scrambled backward, eyes wide, as a huge, dark figure appeared behind Tyler.

"Cruce," she whispered, her heart pounding rapidly.

"Sophie." Cruce's voice was everything she'd remembered and more; it swept over her in a loving caress, soothed her frayed nerves, blanketed her in security. He moved around Tyler, and as he entered the moonlight, she realized he wasn't a shadow at all. It was *him*, in the flesh, real, solid, and majestic.

Cruce leaned down, offering her a hand.

"What the fuck is this?" Tyler demanded. "What the fuck is that thing? I killed it!"

Sophie ignored Cruce's hand and leapt to her feet, throwing her arms around him. She pressed her face to his chest, willing his warmth into her. Fresh tears stung her eyes. "I thought I lost you."

Cruce enfolded her in his embrace, one of his big hands smoothing her tousled hair. "I cannot be so easily taken from you, Josephine Davis. *Sophie.*"

"Get this shit off me!" Tyler shouted, voice high with fear.

Cruce turned toward Tyler, and Sophie turned her head to look at the man she'd once called her husband.

Tyler's eyes were wild with fear, the cords on his neck stood out, and perspiration had beaded on his skin despite the chill in the air. Thick vines were wrapped around each of his arms, keeping them spread to either side.

"You are diseased, mortal," Cruce said.

Wood creaked all around, and before Sophie's eyes, vines sprouted and crept along the nearby trunks. The tendrils binding Tyler pulled taut, lifting him off the ground. He cried out in pain. The branches overhead slowly dipped toward him, their leafless tips sinking into the skin of his arms, producing tiny, gleaming droplets of blood.

"Disease must be purged, to ensure the health of the forest," Cruce continued. "To ensure the safety of its lady." He dipped his head, brushing his lips over Sophie's hair. "Close your eyes, Josephine."

Sophie stared at Tyler. His angry, crazed, terrified eyes locked with hers, pleading, accusing, *hating*.

For once, *he* was the victim. *He* was the one without power. He'd spent years manipulating her, controlling her, dominating her, using his size and strength against her. And finally, Tyler had encountered something he could not overcome. Something he could not control.

He'd come here to hurt her again, and he'd tried to take Cruce from her—had *killed* her mate before her very eyes. And, even if he would've let her survive the night, she had no doubt Tyler would have eventually murdered her.

What kind of person was Sophie if she allowed his torture to continue? If she allowed him to be killed?

And if she told Cruce to let him go? Tyler would hang over her forever, a shadow to haunt her subconscious, a specter from her past that would never allow her to feel wholly safe. Even

Cruce couldn't fully cancel out that feeling, that fear...not after this. Were Tyler to overcome his obsession with Sophie, to let her go, what would he do to the next woman he targeted? Because there would be another. People like him didn't change, didn't stop. She couldn't live knowing that she'd allowed him to hurt someone else the same way he'd hurt her.

No matter which choice was the right one, Sophie knew what she wanted. She knew what had to be done.

Sophie closed her eyes and buried her face against Cruce's chest.

Cruce caressed her hair and pressed another soft kiss to her head.

"You fucking bitch! You goddamn whore!" Tyler screamed. "Don't you turn away from me!"

Loud creaking sounds came from all around—from the vines, from the trees, even from the ground beneath her feet— and Sophie felt immense, indescribable power flowing through the air. Cruce's body warmed further, and she sank against it. Tyler's hateful words became frantic, frightened pleading before descending into agonized screams.

She kept her eyes closed through the wet tearing sounds. Kept her eyes closed as bones popped and snapped, and something splattered on the forest floor. Kept them closed as Tyler released his final, gurgling breath.

Cruce turned away from Tyler, leading Sophie with him, and took her face in his hands. She finally opened her eyes to look up at him.

"It is done, Josephine," he said softly.

Sophie said nothing as she wrapped her arms around Cruce's neck and held him tight. Her body trembled, both from what she'd heard and from the cold. But it was done. It was over. Tyler would never hurt her again.

She was truly free.

· · ·

CRUCE'S FOREST thrummed with life all around, and he felt it as clearly as he felt his own body. His connection with his domain hadn't been this solid since before he was cursed. It filled him with power he'd not tasted in many decades, and magic coursed through his veins like liquid fire. But the thrill of his restored power—and the mystery of why it had returned—was secondary to his relief.

He gathered Sophie in his arms and lifted her off her feet, carrying her toward the cabin. Though he felt the network of roots running underfoot, though he once again possessed the ability to travel through them, he had no desire to do so. All Cruce wanted was to hold her, to feel her against him.

The first night he'd truly shared with Sophie had nearly become the night he'd lost her. All his power could not change that; it was a *what-if* that would linger in his mind for ages to come, a reminder that his arrogance counted for nothing in this world or any other. Assuming he could protect her was not the same as keeping her safe. The latter required dedication, humility, and effort, and he would never take her wellbeing for granted again. He would never allow himself to grow complacent.

She clung to him so tightly as he walked that it seemed she feared he'd vanish if she let go.

Would he?

His memory remained intact when it came to those final moments—he'd died. He'd felt his own life force fade to nothingness. A bullet had pierced his mortal heart, and he had not survived.

He'd awoken in a daze on the forest floor shortly after. The only thing that had cut through his disorientation was Sophie's absence. His initial panic had nearly blinded him to the fact that his senses were wide open; he could feel Tyler and Sophie in his forest, had known exactly where they were. He'd feared he would be too late, and his only goal upon approaching them had been to pry Tyler's focus away from her.

The cabin's windows were dark when Cruce emerged from the trees and entered the lot in front it. Silver moonlight illuminated the area, bathing everything in a glow rich with magic and power. This was the night when the veil between worlds was at its thinnest. When anything seemed possible.

He gently lowered her onto her feet, though he did not relinquish his hold.

She tilted her head back and met his gaze, her dark eyes shining. He sensed her life force, strong and pure, but he did not hunger for it. Though the hollowness within him was gone, his need for her had only grown.

Cruce cupped her face, stroking his thumbs over her cheeks. He gritted his teeth when she winced; the flesh on one side of her face was tight and beginning to swell. Were it possible, Cruce would have ripped Tyler apart all over again for the pain he'd inflicted on Sophie.

Slowly, he ran his hands down her neck and over her shoulders to curl his fingers around her slender arms. Her bare skin was marred by scratches, bruises, and dirt, and the smell of her blood mingled with her lavender and vanilla aroma. But she was still *beautiful*—the most beautiful thing he'd ever seen.

"I have something to give you, Sophie," he said, his voice low and thick. Before he'd met her, he would never have so much as considered what he was about to do. "Something very precious to me…but not as precious as you are."

She settled her palms on his chest. Her fingers were cold, but their touch sent white-hot fire throughout his being. Her lips curled in a small smile. "You've already given me more than I could have wanted. You're *alive*."

"The curse has been broken," he said; he didn't understand how, or why, but its weight had been lifted from him fully. He was Lord of the Forest again.

Sophie inhaled sharply, eyes widening. "Does that mean you won't...disappear? That you won't return to your shadow form?"

"I believe so. We will await the sunrise together to find out. But before then..." He dipped his head and withdrew from her slightly, moving one of his hands to his chest.

Cruce focused on his essence, which he'd not felt this clearly in so long. He called upon it, willing it out of his body a little at a time, and gathered it on his palm in a golden, glittering orb. The orb bathed Sophie's awed face with its warm, gentle glow. Once it had fully coalesced, he divided it evenly; the orb split in two, and one of the pieces sank back into his skin, suffusing him with his own life force. He presented the remaining half to Sophie.

"I want you to take this and become Lady of the Forest," he said, "that we may belong to one another so long as our domain stands."

Sophie pulled her eyes away from the orb to look up at him. "To be with you? Forever?"

"You will be tied to the forest, as am I. It is not eternity, but it is likely to be a long, long while. If I could promise eternity to you...I would."

"So long as I'm with you, I'll take whatever time I can get."

He hesitated, curling his fingers over the orb. "You must know, Sophie, that you will no longer be human after you accept this. This is my essence, my life force. It will make you into something like me."

She wrapped her fingers around his wrist and drew herself closer. "I don't care. I want this. I want *you*. I love you, Cruce."

A torrent of emotions overwhelmed him, sweeping through his body to constrict his chest and throat. She had just given a name to the complex feelings swirling inside him—*love*. He'd never felt it before because he'd never known *her* before. He'd brushed these feelings off as a craving, a need to possess her, a surge of lust in anticipation of his physical form on this night, but it had ever been so much more.

"And I love you, my Sophie."

At her gentle guidance, he extended his arm and pressed his palm to her chest, easing the orb of essence into her heart. She tilted her head back as the glow spread across her skin, its gold overpowering the silver light of the moon. She closed her eyes and parted her lips to release a soft exhalation. The magic whirled around her, whirled *through* her, and solidified her place as the other half of his heart. And he could *feel* her; she thrummed in his awareness like she was an extension of him, part of the same whole and yet still herself, still Sophie.

She finally eased and opened her eyes. They were a bright, honeyed amber now, glowing faintly in the night, but they were undoubtedly hers—they carried all her experiences, all her uniqueness. Her skin emitted a soft light of its own, and her auburn tresses were like shimmering fire.

Cruce dropped to his knees before her, gazing into her eyes. "My lady."

Sophie reached out and ran her fingers—now tipped with delicate claws—through his hair. Her radiant smile outshone the sun on its brightest day. "My lord."

He settled his hands on her hips and tugged her closer. He skimmed his nose over her hair, breathing deep. Her scent filled his senses. "Allow me to worship you until the sun rises and forever after."

"Yes," she breathed.

Cruce slanted his mouth over hers, and she closed her eyes.

He tasted ambrosia from her lips as his hands caressed her body, leaving a blazing trail over her skin. He worshipped her breasts, teased her belly, and stroked her heated sex until she was dripping and quivering in anticipation. Only then did he lay her upon the growing bed of lush grass, soft moss, and blooming flowers that had been summoned by his magic in defiance of the autumn.

Cruce looked down upon his goddess, his Lady of the Forest, his Sophie, and he knew he would always want more of her. Eternity could not satisfy his craving for his mate.

EPILOGUE

"OH MY GOD, Soph, did you see?" Kate asked the instant her bright, smiling face appeared on the laptop screen.

Sophie's brows rose in surprise as she placed the device on the coffee table and sat down on the sofa. "See what?"

"*Her Dark Lover* hit the charts! You're number five on the USA Today Bestseller list."

"You're kidding."

"Hell no, I'm not. Everyone is raving about it, even the ladies in my book group—who freaking loved your book."

Sophie sat back against the cushions, stunned speechless. It'd been years since she'd released a new book. She'd been sure her old readers had forgotten about her after all this time. Her novels had sold decently in the past, but those wholesome stories, while sexy, were tame compared to her latest book. *Her Dark Lover* was about a shadow creature seducing a sweet, innocent heroine who came to welcome the carnal delights he bestowed upon her.

The book had been inspired by Cruce. He'd been exactly what she needed to find that spark again. And what better a love story to tell than your own?

"What...have the reviews said?" Sophie asked, nervously smoothing her hands over the skirt of her dress.

Kate snorted. "Other than a few pearl-clutchers, everyone loves it. I really think you found your niche, Soph. The book is *amazing*. Steve has definitely benefitted from me reading it." She leaned closer, grinning wide, and propped her chin on her cupped hands. "Sooo...when's the next one coming out?"

Sophie laughed. "I'm working on it."

"Well, your biggest fan—and if you haven't already guessed, that's me—is waiting with bated breath."

"I love you."

"I love you too."

Something glittered on Kate's finger, drawing Sophie's attention.

"Kate is that..." Sophie tilted her head and leaned closer to the screen, eyes rounding, and her jaw dropped. "Is that an engagement ring?"

Kate lifted her head with a delighted squeal as she brought the ring closer to the camera. "It is."

The ring was as simple as it was elegant, with two intertwining diamond-studded bands connecting and to circle the larger diamond at the center. It sparkled, fragmenting the light into tiny rainbows.

"It's beautiful!" Sophie said.

Kate lowered her hand and looked at the ring. Her features softened, and she smiled. "He asked me last night, actually."

"Congratulations!"

"It's kind of crazy. I mean, we just started dating seven months ago, but I just...I just knew he was the one, you know? He's so sweet and funny, and his *kids*! Oh Soph, his girls are the greatest. I love them all so much, and they love me, and...and I just..." Kate ran her hand through her hair, brows drawn. "They have such a shitty mom. I really don't want to fuck this up."

"You won't. You're the most caring person I know, Kate. You

deserve this, and I'm so happy for you. And Steve is crazy about you."

"It was that superheroine Halloween costume. I'm telling you, Sophie, the sexy costumes always deliver."

Sophie laughed. "You did look pretty damn hot in it."

"Speaking of hot…" Kate grinned. "Let me see!"

"See what?"

"Oh, you know exactly what I'm talking about. Let me see *you*."

Sophie looked at the small image of herself in the corner of the screen. It felt like looking at an old photo of herself, one from another lifetime—and she supposed it really was a version of her from another lifetime. Her glamour made her look exactly as she had before Cruce shared his life force with her, but…that wasn't Sophie anymore. Not truly.

Well, not except for the happiness that shone in her eyes.

Even though Kate already knew—and what a conversation *that* had been—it was hard for Sophie to let her glamour down, even in front of her dearest friend. She was aware more than ever now of the divide between the mortal world and the super-natural one she'd stepped into with Cruce. The number one rule was not to expose herself to humans. That was usually easy, as the cabin rarely received visitors, and both Cruce and Sophie sensed the approach of anyone within their forest.

Those psychic senses still creeped her out, but she was learn-ing. Learning to understand and control all the power she'd gained. Until she was more comfortable with her role as Lady of the Forest, she was keeping away from humans as much as she could—even though her mortal half allowed her to leave the forest.

But this wasn't any human, it was Kate, the woman who had saved Sophie's life. And Kate had seen it before.

"Where are Steve and the girls?" Sophie asked. The last thing she needed was for Steve or one of his daughters to suddenly walk into the room and see the real Sophie. Though she could easily explain it away as a filter or say she was dressed up for cosplay, it was best to avoid such situations all together.

"He took them out to pick up some candy for movie night tonight. You're safe."

"Okay." Taking in a deep breath, Sophie closed her eyes. Her skin tingled as she willed away the glamour. It was immensely easier to dispel than it was to summon, especially during the first couple months after her transformation. Learning to maintain it had been a test of willpower.

"Wow," Kate said. "I still can't get over how beautiful you are."

Sophie opened her eyes as warmth flooded her cheeks.

"I mean, you were gorgeous before, but now... You're just otherworldly. And you positively glow—for obvious reasons. Your man is one lucky son of a bitch."

"It is not luck. We were fated," Cruce rumbled as he strode across the room toward Sophie. He rarely glamoured himself, and Sophie didn't think she'd ever get used to seeing *human* Cruce. Tall, powerfully built, bronze skinned, but no pointed ears, glowing eyes, antlers, or claws. No fur or hooves. That long, pale hair was closer to blond than silver.

And as much as she loved how his muscular body pushed his partially open button-down shirt and blue jeans to their limits, she'd always prefer him in his natural state—buck-ass naked and wholly unashamed about it.

Cruce leaned over Sophie, hooked a finger under her chin, and tilted her face up toward his, forcing her to meet his gaze. "No luck, but there is no end to my gratitude."

She smiled, and her heart quickened as it always did when he was near. Though his glamour masked his eyes, making them the gray of an autumn sky, it did not hide the desirous light gleaming within them. Warmth bloomed between her thighs. It didn't matter how often they made love, she needed him like she needed air to breathe.

She reached up, stroked his jaw, and threaded her fingers into his hair, aching to draw him closer, to feel his mouth upon hers, to taste him on her lips and tongue, to—

"Well, hellooooo there, handsome," Kate said. "Nice of you to join us."

Sophie blinked, and her fingers clenched Cruce's hair. The warmth that had permeated her core swept up to fill her cheeks. In that moment, she'd forgotten Kate was there.

The fire in Cruce's eyes didn't waver, and he didn't look away from Sophie as he replied, "Hello, Kate Morris."

"You're so creepy when you say my name like that."

Sophie chuckled. She'd thought the same thing when she and Cruce first met and he'd always called her Josephine Davis —not that she'd felt that way for long. Hearing her name in his deep, raspy, rumbling voice was thrill of which she would never tire.

He grunted and turned his head slightly to look at the computer screen. "Why have you sought audience with the Lady of the Forest, Kate Morris?"

Kate rolled her eyes. "Why do you have to be so formal?"

"She called to congratulate me about my book." Sophie poked Cruce in the center of his chest. "And I love hearing from Kate no matter the reason, so be nice."

"Yeah, so take that! Besides, Sophie and I are basically sisters, so that kind of makes you my brother-in-law."

Cruce's eyebrows sank, and he narrowed his eyes. "Brother in what law? I am not beholden to your human rules, Kate Morris." He glanced at Sophie again, and his features softened. "Yet I am powerless but to obey my mate's command."

Kate laughed and grinned. "There are a lot of guys out there who could stand to learn a thing or two from you. But actually, I'm glad you're around, because there's something I wanted to ask both of you. Do you have a minute, Lord of the Forest? No trees to babysit or anything right now?"

Cruce scoffed. "Trees are largely self-sufficient. I find it is humans that require the most observation." He slipped his strong arms under Sophie and scooped her off the couch, seating himself in the place she'd just occupied.

She might have protested had he not settled her sideways on his lap and held her against his broad chest. His spicy, earthy scent filled her nose—arousing, comforting, *right*—and she relaxed against him. He wrapped his arms around her, resting his big hand possessively upon her rounded belly. As though sensing him, her baby shifted within her womb, reaching out to touch him. Cruce's fingers flexed.

Seven months. That was how far along she was. Seven months since that first night they'd come together on Halloween, when Cruce had been made mortal, seven months since she'd become the Lady of the Forest.

Sophie's memory of the day they'd found out she was pregnant was one of the fondest memories in her life. She'd felt something within her for weeks after that Halloween full moon, something warm and precious, but she hadn't realized what it was until she'd awoken one morning with Cruce lying on his stomach between her legs. That in itself hadn't been unusual— he often woke her with his tongue between her thighs. But that time had been different. His hands had been cradling her hips, his ear had been pressed to her belly, and his eyes had been closed.

She'd thought him asleep until he'd opened his eyes and looked up at her. His gaze had shone brighter than she'd ever seen, and his joy had been so immense that it had washed over her in a wave.

"You are with child, my Sophie," he'd said. "*My* child."

And she'd known immediately that he was correct. The spark of warmth she'd felt inside her hadn't merely been part of her new powers—it was the life force of their child. And as she'd lain there with her mate, she'd felt their baby's heartbeat for the first time, so small and soft and fast, the fluttering of a butterfly's wings.

She'd thought Cruce had shown her just how deep and powerful love could be, but that morning had expanded Sophie's love into something impossible to measure, impossible to contain.

Cruce brushed his lips over her forehead. "Our child is strong, and she is eager to enter the world." His words were steeped in the warmth and affection. "All the forest will sing in welcome when the day arrives."

Sophie smiled and placed her hand upon Cruce's. It was so small in comparison, tipped with dainty, but strong claws.

Kate cleared her throat. "I mean, I could...call back later?"

"Speak, Kate." Cruce's voice vibrated into Sophie through his chest. "Ask your question that I may return my attentions to the savoring of my sweet mate."

Kate fanned her face with her hand. "Well damn. Now I can't wait until Steve gets home."

Sophie laughed, skimming her fingers over the roots of his unseen antlers and combing them through his hair. "What'd you want to ask us?"

"So, Steve and I have been talking about dates and arrangements and all that. And we don't want a big thing, just close friends and family. But I was wondering if we could have the wedding there next spring?" She smiled cheekily. "With a fairy tale theme?"

"Oh my God, Kate, that would be so pretty! I can already imagine what the cake will look like. We could hang lights in the branches and make a lighted pathway for you to walk down." Excitement thrummed through Sophie.

She'd never planned a wedding before, and she couldn't wait to help arrange her best friend's. Though she considered herself married to Cruce, their joining had been a simple but magical affair, something that had happened spontaneously, and it was on a level so deep and spiritual it still seemed unreal sometimes. And she and Tyler had been wed in a courthouse by a judge without ceremony.

Sophie stilled.

Tyler.

She hadn't thought of him in months, not since his bones had been discovered by a local hunter. When the remains had been identified as Tyler's, the sheriff and a couple reporters had turned up on Sophie's doorstep to ask questions. Lots of questions.

Maintaining her glamour that soon after her transformation had been difficult, especially while she was being overwhelmed by *feeling* the entire forest and all its creatures, but Cruce's steady guidance had seen her through the challenges. Fortunately, she'd had time to calm herself since the attack on Halloween before speaking with the authorities—and the circumstances of Tyler's death, paired with his criminal record, had absolved her of suspicion.

The official story had been close to the truth. A deranged, obsessed man, recently released from prison after nearly beating his wife to death, had driven into Raglan in a car rented under a false name and begun asking around town for Josephine. When he discovered her whereabouts, he'd driven to the forest, parked the rental where it was hidden from the road, and headed for her cabin on foot...with gun in hand.

But he'd been mauled by a bear before ever reaching that cabin. His gun had been emptied, suggesting an attempt to defend himself, but there'd been little left of his dismembered remains by the time they were found. It had been considered a potential tragedy averted; no one had any question of Tyler's motives for trying to sneak to the cabin with a firearm.

The story had traveled around town quickly, and Sophie had

been swarmed with cards, calls, and gift baskets, with containers of casseroles and pies—the little town had gone out of their way to make the poor woman who'd come here to escape feel welcome and safe.

Doris had been giving Sophie her employee discount at the grocery store ever since, despite Sophie's protests. The older woman still felt guilty for telling Tyler where the cabin was, having taken his story about being Sophie's deployed husband at face value.

"I have no wish to invite a group of unfamiliar humans into my forest," Cruce said, drawing Sophie back to the present.

"Well, considering Sophie will be my Maid of Honor, she will need to attend," Kate said. "So she'd have to, you know, leave your forest. *Alone.*"

Even though she wasn't looking at him, Sophie felt the blistering intensity of Cruce's scowl.

"Unacceptable," he snarled.

"Then I guess the only option is to have the wedding there. Great! It's all settled."

"You try my patience, mortal. This is my domain, and I—"

Unable to hold back her laughter, Sophie gently swatted Cruce's shoulder. "Be nice. If it weren't for Kate, I wouldn't even be here."

He growled and held Sophie a little closer. "Fine."

Kate grinned. "Awesome! I knew you'd come around. So I was thinking—"

Sophie yelped and giggled when Cruce's arm tightened, clamping her securely in place as he leaned forward, reached out, and pressed the button to end the call.

Grinning, Sophie looked at her mate. "I guess I'll talk to her about it later."

"Much later," Cruce rumbled, sitting back. He lifted a hand to her face, cradling her cheek in his big palm, and stared down at her. His glamour melted away. Those long, many pronged antlers formed atop his head, his eyes sparked with silvery starlight, and his skin took on that golden hue she loved so much. "After I have had my fill of you, my Sophie."

"You always say you'll never have your fill of me," she teased, running her fingertips along his jaw while she pressed her other hand to his bare chest through the opening in his shirt. A needy ache thrummed in her core.

"Then I suppose Kate will be waiting a very long time," he said as he slid her off his lap and deposited her on the couch. Pushing her back against the cushions, he knelt on the floor and placed his hands on her knees. Those hands slid up slowly, lifting her skirt as they moved, creating tantalizing tingles in their wake. "For my thirst for my lady cannot be quenched."

Sophie's breath hitched, eyes never leaving his as he parted her thighs and dipped his head between them. A soft gasp spilled from her lips when his tongue swiped over her sex. He growled and kissed deeper, sliding his palms beneath her to grasp her ass. His fingers tightened, his claws pricking her flesh, as he dragged her closer to his ravenous mouth.

"Cruce," she breathed, lashes fluttering as pleasure suffused her. She tangled her fingers in his hair, urging him closer, desperate for more, more, more.

He was her shadowy lover, her Lord of the Forest. Her seducer, her savior, her mate. Her darkest craving.

And Sophie's appetite was as insatiable as his.

AUTHOR'S NOTE

Thank you so much for reading His Darkest Craving. If you enjoyed it, please consider leaving a review.

And if you'd love to read more of our stories, we have so many more for you to choose from whether you're looking for sexy aliens in disguise on Earth, Krakens on another world, or our more monstrous spider aliens.

We'd also love it if you joined our reader group on FaceBook.

ALSO BY TIFFANY ROBERTS

The Weaver

The Delver

The Hunter

THE CURSED ONES

His Darkest Craving

His Darkest Desire

ALIENS AMONG US

Taken by the Alien Next Door

Stalked by the Alien Assassin

Claimed by the Alien Bodyguard

STANDALONE TITLES

Claimed by an Alien Warrior

Dustwalker

Escaping Wonderland

Yearning For Her

The Warlock's Kiss

Ice Bound: Short Story

ISLE OF THE FORGOTTEN

Make Me Burn

Make Me Hunger

Make Me Whole

Make Me Yours

VALOS OF SONHADRA COLLABORATION

Tiffany Roberts - Undying

Tiffany Roberts - Unleashed

VENYS NEEDS MEN COLLABORATION

Tiffany Roberts - To Tame a Dragon

Tiffany Roberts – To Love a Dragon

ABOUT THE AUTHOR

Tiffany Roberts is the pseudonym for Tiffany and Robert Freund, a husband and wife writing duo. Tiffany was born and bred in Idaho, and Robert was a native of New York City before moving across the country to be with her. The two have always shared a passion for reading and writing, and it was their dream to combine their mighty powers to create the sorts of books they want to read. They write character driven sci-fi and fantasy romance, creating happily-ever-afters for the alien and unknown.